FEATHERS
IN
WATER

D. R. Cassady

D. R. Cassady: www.DwainWrites.com

Cover image by Getcovers.
Author photo by Becky Franks.

This is a work of fiction. All names, characters, places, and companies are purely a product of the author's imagination or are used fictitiously. Any resemblance to any actual person, place, business, or event is purely coincidental. Please enjoy the read.

ISBN: Paperback: 978-1-7361395-6-1
        eBook: 978-1-7361395-7-8

ACKNOWLEDGMENTS

I am exceedingly grateful to the folks who helped bring this novel into existence. Kayla Brown, B. J. Myers-Bradley, Pam Parks, and Tammy Walker were instrumental in reading through the manuscript, hunting down typos, and providing feedback to greatly improve the novel. I really appreciate their time and insights. Merilyn Guerry is a grammar ninja, and I am grateful to her for editing the manuscript so carefully. I am also indebted to Becky Franks for the author photo and the designer at Getcovers.com for the cover. Their artistic skills are wonderful.

Most of all, I am grateful to each of you who read this novel, letting me share this story with you. Understanding that we are all created by the great power of Love and valued for who we are is an important message that I hope to communicate through this novel. I hope that comes across for you. I welcome your feedback at
dwain.cassady@dwainwrites.com.

After you are done, please leave a review on the site from which you purchased the book. Thanks again and enjoy the read!

FEATHERS
IN
WATER

Chapter 1

Friday, October 12, 2018

It was the best year of my life! I was a high school senior! I flicked my fingers through my brown pixie hairdo, straightened my posture, and stepped out of the school building like I owned the place. And that day, I felt like I did. I saw my two best friends and hurried over.

"Hey, Myra! Hey, Jaynie! You are going to the game tonight, right?"

"Well, I have to be there," Jaynie, the captain of the color guard, scolded.

"I'm going with Kyle. He asked me last night," Myra said with a wiggle of excitement.

"You always have a date!" I laughed.

"Yeah, how do you line up so many guys?" Jaynie asked.

"Just lucky, I guess," Myra smiled. "How about you, Willow? Are you going with someone special?" She grinned even bigger.

"No, it will be just me, as usual."

"Why don't you ever have any dates? You're too nice and too pretty never to be asked out," Myra pointed out.

"Yeah, are you a lesbian or something?" Jaynie laughed.

Their laughter receded, and I felt I was falling down a dark tunnel. The light dimmed. Myra and Jaynie seemed to be moving farther and farther away. I could still hear them laughing. One, Myra maybe, said something about helping to find me a date. I tried to respond but couldn't. Finally, the circle of light closed, and I was in my own dark world.

The next thing I knew, I was walking from my car toward the house. *I don't remember driving home.* I opened the door and headed straight for my room, ignoring Mom's greetings and questions about the day. As I closed the door, "Aren't you supposed to be at tennis practice?" filtered through to my consciousness.

I fell onto my bed. *What is going on? What is this earthquake in my soul.* Our cat, gray with a white chest and named Tazmania, jumped onto the bed and rubbed her chin to mine. "Hey, Taz." I stroked her back. The truth began to emerge from the darkness.

"It's me. Are you OK?"

The knock and the voice of my twin brother, Will, shocked me. I felt like I was emerging from fog and looked at the clock. *Five-thirty! How could it be that late?* I shook my head to help bring myself back to reality. "Come in."

I sat up as Will came in. "Close the door."

"Are you OK?" he asked again. "Mom said you've been in here all afternoon. She said you didn't say anything when she knocked and asked about you."

Will, a five-foot eleven-inch bundle of energy, stood still. I could see the concern on his face. He is my rock. He ran his fingers through his unruly brown hair, waiting for me to respond.

"I think I'm lesbian."

"What? No way! What makes you say that?"

"It just hit me this afternoon. Myra, Jaynie, and I were talking about dates, and Jaynie joked about my being a 'lesbian.'" I made air quotes. "The ground seemed to open and swallow me. I've been lying here thinking about it all afternoon. I think she's right." The heaviness of the revelation weighed on my spirit.

"Look, I know you don't date a lot, but that doesn't mean you're a lesbian. You just haven't found a guy that's good enough for you. That's going to be a tall order, you know."

"I don't know, Will. It just seems to fit."

"Well, you can't let your whole life be determined by one off-handed comment. Besides, we have a football game to go to! Do you want to ride with Sandra and me?"

"I'm not sure I feel up to going," I moped.

"You'll feel better once you get there. I'm going to get showered. I wish you had been at practice today. I had to play Larry. He's terrible!" Will opened the door and looked back, "Willow, I think this will take a while for you to sort out. So just get ready and let's go to the game."

"OK." *I know he's right. I'll have to summon the energy somehow.*

I could hear Mom grilling Will from the kitchen. "Well? What's going on with Willow?"

"Someone said something to her at school that hurt her feelings. She'll be OK."

Will is the best! It wasn't a lie, but it wasn't the whole truth, either.

I checked my phone and saw a pile of texts and three missed calls, all from Myra and Jaynie. I texted them back. "Sorry! I had a lot on my mind this afternoon and wasn't feeling well. Better now!" I added a smiley emoji. "See you at the game!"

Thirty minutes later, I heard Will dancing and singing as he came out of his room. When I opened my door, he grabbed me by the hand trying to get me to dance with him.

"I don't feel like dancing," I grumped. I knew it was pointless, though. Will's energy is contagious. My resistance lasted about three seconds, then I was dancing, too. We danced into the kitchen, and Will let go of me and grabbed Mom in a hug.

"I have a date with my sweetie and favorite sister! It's going to be a great night!"

I punched him in the arm. "I'm your only sister!"

"I hope you're feeling better," Mom, whose name is Joyce and who is the source of our brunette hair and brown eyes, said. She was looking me over closely. "I'm sorry someone upset you so."

"I'm better. Thanks, Mom." *I hope she doesn't ask for details.*

We got out without further interrogation. "We can take my Jeep."

"That's OK. Let's take my car so you won't look like a chauffeur," he said as he pressed the fob to unlock his Prius.

He pulled into Sandra's driveway and hopped out to knock on the door. Sandra came bouncing out before he got there and waved at me as I was moving from the front seat to the back. Will took Sandra's hand, and I heard him say, "I brought Willow. I hope that's OK."

"No, that's fine. I sort of expected she'd be with us. You bring her about half the time, anyway."

"Is it that much?" Will asked sheepishly. *Now I really feel like a third wheel.*

"Yep! But that's OK. I like Willow." With that, we headed for the football game.

We parked in the school lot farthest from the field. Most of the students parked there because it was easier to get out after the game. It also gave us a chance to walk past Witchaleea's house.

Witchaleea is the name Will had given to the wrinkled, white-haired woman who sat under her carport every home football game and watched. She never moved. She never waved. She never smiled. She just watched from across the road as people made their way toward the football stadium. Will had said that she must be some kind of witch, hence the name Witchaleea.

All the students talked and joked about the woman. She was never seen except on the evenings of home football games. As we walked toward the stadium, I watched her, trying not to stare. I was shocked when our eyes met. Her hand raised ever so slightly.

It took a minute for it to register that she might have just waved. I smiled and waved back but saw no other movement. *Wow! Did that just happen? She waved at me!* I turned to tell Will and Sandra what had happened and discovered I had stopped walking. They had kept going and were leaving me behind.

I hustled to catch up, and the reality of what was about to happen hit. *What am I supposed to do tonight? Do I tell anyone what I've been thinking?* My stomach did a somersault and a wave of queasiness flowed through. *I think that's my answer. I don't have to tell anyone tonight. Just act normal.*

"Hurry up, slacker!" Will's call penetrated my thoughts. I caught up with them and readied my soul to face tonight. We bought our tickets and went through the gates.

Myra came charging over, dragging Kyle by the hand. "Hey, Willow! I'm glad you're feeling better! What was wrong this afternoon?"

I froze. Myra, short and shapely with beautiful jet-black hair that curled and kinked at will, was my best friend. My heart wanted to confide in her so badly. I needed to share what was going on, but I wasn't ready. So I leaned over and whispered a lie into Myra's ear. "Period."

"Girl, you had me worried!" Myra responded. "Come on. Kyle, Ben, and I are sitting in the usual spot."

I hadn't noticed Ben, a pudgy blond who was a math whiz, standing with Kyle. I waved to Will and Sandra, who were headed to talk with some of Sandra's friends, looped my arm through Myra's, and walked with them to the bleachers. As we sat down, the crowd erupted with cheers and yells.

"Did you see that!" Kyle hollered over the noise. "Jason just caught a 50-yard pass!"

"No, I missed it," I called back. *It's hard to watch a football game when my whole being has just been turned upside down.* The excitement calmed, and people sat back down. Sitting next to Myra, I tried to focus on the game, but my mind kept drifting back to this afternoon. Cheers, the occasional whistle, and the general constant motion of people moving about faded as I thought about how I had felt when Jaynie made her comment.

Could it really be possible? Did I just overreact? What does this mean for my life? Somehow, sitting amid the crowd afforded me the chance to disappear and look deep into my heart. *I'm so confused! Do I dare talk to Myra? Maybe she could help me sort this out. Maybe I'll ask her if we could talk later.*

I was about to lean over to ask Myra when someone bumped my left elbow. I was surprised to see Ben lowering himself to sit beside me. *He has two drinks in his hand. What does that mean. Oh no!*

He looked at me and said, "I thought you might like a hot chocolate."

Time froze. I looked to my right and saw Myra grinning at me. *What to do? What to do? I don't know! Do I accept the drink?* I swallowed, summoned a smile, and said, "Sure! Thanks, Ben!" I took a sip and was relieved that Ben's eyes returned to the game.

As the game progressed, the temperature dropped. *I'm glad I brought my jacket!* I pulled it out from under me and started wiggling into it. Ben reached over and helped me get the second sleeve on.

"Thanks."

"You're welcome. Umm, would you like to go get an ice cream after the game?" he asked timidly.

My heart turned a flip. A tsunami of feelings flooded my soul. *What exactly am I feeling?* Flattered, excited, scared, but not repulsed were some that surfaced. Finally, the feeling that seemed to take precedence was fear. *I don't want to hurt his feelings.* So I said, "Sure. OK."

The fourth quarter dragged out. Our team was ahead in the battle on the field, but I was focused on the battle in my heart. *Why did I say, "Yes?" What was I thinking? The last thing I need right now is a date! OK, heart, calm down. It's just ice cream. He seems like a nice guy. Maybe Will was right. Maybe I am overreacting. Let's just see what happens tonight.*

When I felt I had regained some control over my heart, I leaned over to Myra, "Ben asked me to go for ice cream after the game."

"Yay! Way to go, girl! Wait, you are going, aren't you?" I could tell she really hoped I was. It was then that it hit me. *She set this up!*

"I am, and I suspect you had something to do with this."

"Would I do such a thing?" she asked, grinning broadly.

I punched her in the arm, and she laughed.

With a loud roar, the crowd stood and cheered. The game was over, and we had won!

"Where would you like to go?" Ben asked after the noise subsided.

"I don't know, but we have a tradition that we have to do before I can leave. Myra and I always go and congratulate Jaynie on her performance."

Ben looked surprised.

"You and Kyle talk guy stuff. We'll be right back."

Walking back with Jaynie and Myra, I decided that we might as well go to my favorite spot for ice cream. When Ben asked again, I said, "How about Bellini's? I love their gelato."

"I've never been there, but it sounds good,"

"I have to let Mom and Will know that I'm going with you," I explained as I wrote a text.

It was 11:15 when we pulled into the driveway. "Thanks for going with me tonight," he said.

"Thank you for the gelato! It was great!" *That was a bit awkward.*

Ben walked me to the door and held out his hand. I put my hand in his. *I hope he doesn't want to kiss me!*

"Maybe we can go out again sometime," he suggested, looking at the ground.

"Maybe so."

He smiled and let go of my hand. "Good night."

Will was already home and watching TV with our parents in the den. I poked my head in. "Hey! I'm home."

"Hey! I hear you had a date tonight," he prompted.

"Sort of. We just went for gelato after the game."

"So you took him to your favorite place!" Will grinned, eyeing the cup. I had finished eating it on the way to the house since Ben wolfed his down so quickly.

"Oh hush! It was just a short date." My cheeks flushed as I walked around the couch for good night hugs. "I'm tired. I'm going on to bed."

Lying down, I began to process the day's events. *OK, I sort of enjoyed going out with Ben. He was nice. Not very talkative. What would I have done if he tried to kiss me? Ugh! I'm glad he didn't! There were definitely no fireworks. Could I really be more attracted to girls than guys?*

All the thoughts and feelings swirling around made me tired. *I'll worry about this tomorrow.* Soon after that, I drifted off to sleep.

Chapter 2

Sunday, October 14, 2018

Mom knocked and poked her head in. "It's time to get up, sleepy head! You have an hour to get ready for Sunday school." I opened my eyes and forced myself to sit up. I heard the same call at Will's door down the hall. I pulled my diary out of the nightstand and read what I had written last night.

My spirit is confused. Am I lesbian, or am I straight? Why is it hard to figure out? While Will and I were playing tennis, there was a couple playing next to us. He was trying to teach her the game. I thought she was quite cute. Him, not so much. Is that a clue? Will said that he thinks this will take a long time for me to sort out. It looks like he's right.

I put down the diary and looked into the mirror. "Lord, help me to figure this out, please," I prayed. Will poked his head in.

"Hey!"

"Hey, yourself."

"Are you up for this?" he asked.

"Up for what?"

"Sunday school and church."

"What do you mean?"

"You do know that Roger is against homosexuality."

"Will! Wait, you're right! He has said that. What am I going to do?" Will just opened another pressure point: our youth minister.

"Absolutely nothing!" he said. "It's none of his business. We shall just carry on as usual."

"OK. You're right again. I may try to talk to Myra today, though."

"That's a good idea. You know I am for you no matter what you decide…. or maybe I should say discover."

"Thanks, Will! You're the best brother ever!" I hustled over to hug him.

Will and I left our parents in the hallway and headed to the youth room. Roger Giles, the youth minister, was playing the guitar and leading a song when we got there. His blond hair hung down, covering his blue eyes and chiseled face while he played. We slipped in beside Myra and Jaynie. When the song ended, Roger prayed and led the class through a lesson on how to share your faith without annoying people.

With the lesson over, Roger said, "Let us pray. Father, we love you very much and are grateful for all your blessings. Please help us not to keep your love to ourselves but to share it with all those people out there who are living in sin and brokenness and need to find you. Amen."

Conversations flowed over the room. Will hopped over to talk with some of his friends. I stayed to talk with Myra and Jaynie. Jaynie looked at her phone and said, "I have to go! We're going to visit my aunt and uncle today!" She hustled out of the room.

I guess that's the sign I was looking for. I grabbed Myra's hand and whispered, "I need to talk to you."

"OK," Myra said.

"But not here. Let's go out to the pavilion." I took off, trusting she would follow.

Myra caught up with me and said, "Didn't Roger look dreamy today? I like the way he is wearing his hair! To tell you the truth, it was hard for me to concentrate on the lesson!"

Normally I would have just agreed with Myra, but today I thought for a moment. *No, I don't really see anything that wonderful about him. I guess he is handsome but certainly not distracting.* I mustered a response and said, "I'm sorry you were having trouble concentrating."

"Oh my! Something serious must be going on," she said.

The pavilion was nestled under some old oak trees in a grassy area. The leaves filtered the light, leaving a dappled pattern of light and shadow as we walked. I felt I was moving between worlds in the same dappled pattern.

I leaned against a table, and Myra hopped up beside me. "You look troubled," she prompted.

"Do you remember when I freaked out last Friday?" *I need to ease into this.*

"Yeah! You had to run because your period started."

"Actually, that was a lie. Do you remember what Jaynie said?"

"No. Would you quit beating around the bush and tell me what's up?" she said, cutting to the chase.

"I know she was teasing, but Jaynie said, 'Are you a lesbian?' It hit me like a ton of bricks that she might be right."

"Are you saying that you're lesbian?"

"I think so. I don't know. It's so hard to figure out."

"But you went out with Ben after the game."

"I know. I'm so confused. He seemed nice, and I didn't want to hurt his feelings. But there is no attraction there."

"What about Roger?" Myra asked.

"What about Roger?"

"Doesn't he make your heart flutter?"

"No, I can't say that he does."

"This is serious," she said with a chuckle.

"What am I going to do?" I buried my face in my hands.

"First of all, you're going to be you. Just be you. You're a wonderful person, and God created you just the way you are for a special reason."

"But I don't want to be different. It will cause so many problems. I want to be like everyone else… like you."

"Willow, the world couldn't take two of me," she said with a grin. "But it would be a sad place without you. You are who you are, and that is OK. We'll figure this out together."

Piano music floated on the air. "We're late for church! I'll get a scolding. Come on, Willow."

Myra dragged me in, and we settled into a back pew so as not to cause too much of a disturbance and, hopefully, to avoid drawing the attention of our parents. Except during the singing, my attention drifted and my heart and mind wrestled. I totally tuned out the sermon.

I think I really know the answer. That's why I'm always more interested in girls than guys. But, I have always been taught that homosexuality, or bi or trans or any of the others that don't fit the norm of a man and woman married, is wrong. God, I'm sitting in your house thinking about this. What do you think? I tried to tune back in and listen. I hadn't even noticed the tear rolling down my cheek. Myra reached over and squeezed my hand.

A wave of acceptance flowed through my heart, and a few more tears formed. It confused me. *Is this a sign from God? Am I just coming to terms with who I am? Is it just the support of a dear friend? Lord, I am one hot mess. I hope you will lead me through this.*

Myra bumped my elbow, and I noticed everyone was standing for the closing hymn. I had not heard a word of the sermon.

"Pastor Stevens is going to think she preached a really moving sermon," Myra leaned in and whispered.

I spent the afternoon in my room, trying to study. It was almost as bad as trying to listen to the sermon. I finally gave up and pulled out my diary.

It appears that I am not the person I thought I was. I am different. I am new. I will have to get to know this new person living in my skin. I'm scared. Is this new me the real me? Am I just having some kind of crisis? It is a crisis, that's for sure. But is it real? My heart seems to think so. If so, am I headed for a lifetime of rejection? Will you reject me, too, God? Coming out of the cocoon is frightening and exhilarating at the same time. Lord, please help me. You won't really abandon me, will you?

I heard the familiar sound of Will's feet pounding down the hall. He knocked.

"Come in."

Poking his head in, he said, "It's time to go to youth group."

I'm not sure what my expression was, but he said, "What's wrong? You look… tense."

"I was just going over and over my new-found mess."

"Well, quit sitting there spinning your gears and let's spin some wheels to the church! It's your turn to drive." He pulled me from the bed and out the door.

Myra came scampering up to the Jeep as I parked. "Hey, Willow-Will!"

"Hey, Myra," we said at the same time.

Linking her arm in mine, she said softly, "Are you OK? You look stressed."

"That's what Will said. I guess it shows. I'm still wrestling with who I am."

"Well whoever you are, I like you!" she said with a big smile.

"Thanks!" I hugged her arm. "I needed to hear someone say that."

Roger was leading the group through the first song when we entered the youth room. *Late again!* We joined in the song and took our seats.

After the singing and a prayer, Roger started the lesson. "Today we are going to talk about the power of love. God's main call on our lives is to love people. In fact, God wants us Christians to love everybody on the planet, even criminals. But the reason God wants us to love these people is not just so we will feel good, but so we can effect change in the person's life.

"If a criminal is convicted of a crime, put in prison, then dumped back out into society, what is going to happen? He or she will probably go right back to crime unless he or she has been impacted by being loved. Love is what can produce a change in the person's life, not punishment. God expects you and me to love the criminal into a better life.

"We hear a lot about homosexuality today," Roger continued. I tensed so suddenly that I wondered if people had noticed. "Our job is to love them, too. God expects us to welcome these folks into the church and show them that we care."

This doesn't sound like the old Roger.

"Because if we can love them and care for them, we have the potential to change them into Godly people."

The sudden force of the anger rising in my heart surprised me. *The real Roger returns.*

"We know that the Bible says that homosexuality is wrong, so we have the opportunity to steer a person toward a life of which God approves only if we love them first. We can't change a person with judgement and shame. That only drives them away. It is love that has the power to change."

I'm sure my face was flushing red. My anger was so hot, I was shaking. *What is going on? I can't stay here! I have to get out!* I rushed out of the room with Roger's words, "Each one of you has the potential to love another person into salvation," chasing me down the hall.

I ran to the pavilion. Pounding my fists on the picnic table, I ranted, "He's right. What am I thinking! I have to be straight. It's wrong not to be."

I heard Myra and Will coming up behind me.

"That's one mad chica!" Myra said.

"Pity the picnic table!" Will responded as they hurried over.

"Um, what's up?" Will asked.

"Roger is right!" I said, wiping the tears dripping off my nose. "I can't be lesbian. I have to be straight. That is the right thing to do."

My phone rang. I snatched it out of my pocket and barked, "Hello!"

"Uh, Willow, it's Ben."

"Hey, Ben."

"I was wondering… Wait, is this an OK time to talk?"

"Yeah. What is it?"

"I was wondering if you would want to go to the homecoming dance with me."

"Sure. That will be great," and I hung up. "See, that wasn't so hard! I'm going to the homecoming dance with Ben. I am normal, just like I'm supposed to be!"

"You also just hung up on him," Will pointed out.

I grunted and called him back. "Hey, Ben. I'm a little stressed right now. Was there anything else we needed to talk about?"

"Just plans for the dance, I guess. But that can wait if you want to."

"Great! Thanks for asking me. I'll talk to you later." I hung up again. "Was that better?"

"Better but really lacking romance," Myra responded.

I grunted again, "I'll work on that later."

"Uh-oh! Here comes Roger," Will noticed as he took off.

"What's wrong?" Roger asked, his eyes oozing concern.

"PMS," Will answered softly. "It's best to just let her get it out of her system." I watched as Roger's mind seemed to short circuit. He started and stopped and then seemed willing to take Will's advice.

"I see. Well, let me know if I can help," he said and hurried toward the church.

Chapter 3

I pulled into the parking lot for the homecoming game.

"I would have been glad to drive," Ben offered.

"It's fine, Ben. I like to drive. Do you think Witchaleea will be in her usual spot?"

"Of course!" Will said as he climbed out of the back seat and offered Sandra a hand.

"I wonder what her story is," I mused.

"They say she murdered her roommate and buried her in the back yard," Ben said. "Every now and then a dog will dig up a human bone and bring it home."

"What? No way!" I said, crinkling my nose in disbelief.

"I bet the bones are still in the house, lying in the bed where she killed her!" Will said spookily.

"EEEWWW! That's gross!" Sandra said.

As we walked toward the stadium, talk turned to the game. "We have to win tonight," Ben said. "It would be embarrassing to lose our homecoming game."

"We beat these guys last year, so I'm sure we can do it again," Will offered.

I stopped directly across from Witchaleea's house. The others kept walking and talking. She smiled and waved, her skeletal hand lifting then slowly floating down to her knee.

I waved back then hurried to catch up. "She waved at me!"

"Who waved at you?" Will asked.

"Witchaleea!" I was grinning.

"No way! I don't believe it!" Will argued, looking back at her. "She has never waved at anyone."

"What can I say?"

"Wow! You must be special!" Ben added.

Conflict rumbled in my soul. I almost lashed out at Ben but realized he was just trying to be nice. My consternation must have shown because Ben said, "I meant special in a good way."

I forced a smile and said, "Thanks! It wasn't what you said. I've had a lot on my mind lately. I promise no more dark thoughts. Let's go win a football game!"

Saturday, Oct.20, 2018

"What time is it?"

"Two thirty-five," Will said.

"We have to go! I have a mission to accomplish before Ben picks me up!"

It was Saturday afternoon before the homecoming dance. "One more serve," He pleaded. Without waiting for my response, he tossed the ball and served it. I hit a fierce backhand that sailed past him.

"That was definitely a state championship worthy shot!" he exclaimed. "If we keep playing like this, I think we can win it this year."

"I totally agree! That will make us the first twins ever to win the state mixed doubles title. I could live with that! Now take me home."

"What is this mission?"

"I'm taking brownies to Witchaleea," I said with a smile.

"Are you crazy?"

"I think she is a lonely old woman who could use some kindness."

"Well, don't let her tie you to the bed where she keeps her roommate's bones!"

I punched him in the arm and hopped into his Prius. At home, I called, "I get the shower first!"

After cutting the brownies, I put six on a paper plate, covering them with cling wrap. I stuck an orange bow on top since Halloween was near and rushed out the door.

As I approached Witchaleea's driveway, my hands began to shake. *Maybe Will was right. Why am I doing this? I should just turn around and go back home.*

I drove past the driveway then smacked my hand on the steering wheel. "This is ridiculous! I made the brownies and came this far. It's not like she can chase me down and drag me into her house. I'm doing it!" I said aloud. I turned around and pulled slowly into the driveway.

I surveyed the old, poorly maintained one-story brick home and its open carport. The yard was a shamble of weeds and overgrown bushes. A little more apprehension sneaked in as I willed myself to open the door and get out. I elected to go to the carport door to avoid wading through the weeds.

I steeled my nerves as I walked to the door. When I reached to knock, the door flew open. Witchaleea was standing there, glaring at me.

"Hi. I brought you…" I froze when she opened the screen and stepped out suddenly, moving faster than I would have expected.

"I know you," the old woman said in a screechy, crackly voice.

"How could you know me? We have never met."

"I see things. I know things. Brownies. You brought brownies!" She snatched the plate like lightning.

"I hope you like them," I said, hoping my astonishment didn't show.

"I like them. Thank you. Your soul is strong and flexible. Like a willow."

"It's funny you should say that. My name is Willow."

"I see things. I know things. Brownies." The old woman turned and closed the door.

I stood with my mouth open, not sure what to do. *Why did she tell me I am like a willow?* A sense of relief flooded over me. *I guess that mission is accomplished.* I hustled home.

The challenge of getting ready for the homecoming dance pushed the thoughts of my encounter with the old woman from my mind. I hustled to put a bit of mousse in my hair, added some make up, and slipped into my dress. I went out into the den for my parents to oooh and ahhh, getting there just before Will came out in his tuxedo.

"You two look marvelous," Mom gushed.

"Wow, you do clean up nicely!" Dad added.

"OK, in front of the fireplace for pictures!" Mom directed while Dad got the camera. On the fifth shot, the doorbell rang.

I started for the door, but Dad, a tall lanky blond, held up his hand. "It's proper for the father to answer the door. You just be patient."

I could hear Ben introducing himself. Dad led him into the den. He was sporting a dark maroon tuxedo that blended perfectly with my ivory dress with its tiny burgundy roses. Ben offered me a wrist corsage.

"Wow! That's beautiful, Ben!" I said and held out my hand. He seemed flummoxed.

"You're supposed to put it on her," Will coaxed.

He slid the corsage onto my wrist. We posed for three more pictures then headed out to pick up Sandra.

I can do this. I slid my hand into Ben's elbow as we walked toward the gym. He seemed to like that. *He's a nice enough guy. I think this will be OK.*

Loud music crashed through the door as Ben held it open. The sound elevated my energy level. Grabbing Ben's hand, I rushed us onto the dance floor. I lost myself in the music and was dancing freely. It dawned on me that I was grinning.

When the song ended, Ben stood there awkwardly then took two steps toward the side of the auditorium. *He's going to sit down!* I grabbed his arm. "I love to dance! Let's stay for the next song."

"OK." I sensed that dancing was not Ben's passion. By the end of the next song, he was sweating. *I guess I'd better give this guy a rest.* I led him off the floor.

Spotting Myra and Kyle, I pulled Ben over to them.

"You are a dancing machine!" Myra said as we hugged.

"You look spectacular!" I said, eyeing Myra's ivory dress that had a subtle leaf pattern. It was stunning next to her ebony skin.

"That's the word I was looking for," Kyle said. "Spectacular!" He leaned down and gave Myra a quick kiss.

"I think Ben needs some punch," I said, and we all went for refreshments.

We talked through two songs, then Myra shouted, "That's our song!" Come on!" She grabbed Kyle's hand. I dragged Ben back onto the dance floor, too.

I swallowed a little too hard when the slow song started. Ben held out his left hand. I willed my hand into his and drew close. I felt stiff at first. *I need to relax. This will be OK.* I focused on the music, and my body began to move fluidly with Ben's. I could see over his shoulder and watched the other couples, some getting a bit too intimate for a public place.

I noticed Susan's low cut dress. Obviously, her partner did, too. He kept stepping back and looking down. By the end of the dance, it dawned on me: *I've been eyeing the girls instead of the guys.* Heaviness settled in. *I have to be happy for Ben's sake.* I forced a smile as we walked off the dance floor.

At the stroke of midnight, the band announced the last song. "We're going to end the night with 'Anti-Hero.' Everybody on the floor! Let's dance!" the lead singer prompted.

I set my cup on the table, relieved. I took Ben's hand and pulled him onto the dance floor. *He looks relieved, too. I hope I haven't ruined his evening.*

Myra's voice crashed into my thoughts. "See you at my house for breakfast!"

"Wouldn't miss it," I called back over the music.

Chapter 4

Sunday, October 21, 2018

When the song ended, I asked Ben, "Are you still up for going to Myra's for breakfast?"

"I'd love to."

We milled around, talking to a few friends, and wandered over to hook up with Will and Sandra.

"It's breakfast time!" Will said, still dancing as he led Sandra to the door. She looked at me and shrugged her shoulders. Her grin told me she liked it, though.

Ben pulled into Myra's driveway at 12:27. "I've got the parent text." I sent Mom a quick text telling her we made it to Myra's safe and sound.

"Do you think they'll still be up when we get home?" Will asked.

"No, but they'll be listening for us!"

Ben put his arm around my waist as we walked to the door. I instinctively stiffened. *You have to chill!* I relaxed and leaned into him briefly.

"I enjoyed dancing with you," he said.

"Me, too." *It wasn't really a lie.*

There were five couples coming to Myra's. They were gathered in the den, cuddling on couches and chairs, the girls looking stiff in their dresses. I found a spot on one of the couches and sat down. Ben sat very close. My anxiety level rose just a bit, but I didn't stiffen up like earlier. *That's progress.* I could hear Myra's parents clanging plates in the kitchen over the hum of couples talking.

"That was an amazing pass last night, Curt!" Kyle said as he and Myra came into the den.

"Thanks," Curt answered, his arm around Jaynie as he perched on the arm of the chair next to her.

"Yeah, he's amazing," Jaynie said.

"It's always nice to win the homecoming game," Myra added.

"I'm glad we won for our senior year," Curt said.

"Yeah, that was almost as good as dancing with my sweetie!" Will said as he gave Sandra a quick hug with the arm that was already around her.

I glanced at Ben. He seemed tense. "Are you OK?"

"Yeah, I'm having a good time."

I understood the tenseness when Ben slid his arm around me. *He was wondering if I would push it away.* I looked at him and saw big question marks in his eyes. I answered with a smile and leaned over against him. *This isn't so bad.*

I looked up and caught Will's gaze. He didn't have to say a word for me to know that he was asking, "Are you OK with that?" It's a twin thing. We can just understand each other.

I gave the slightest nod and knew that he knew I was OK with Ben's arm around me. *It's nice to have a brother who has my back!*

"I worked up an appetite on the dance floor," Will announced.

"You can work up an appetite just by breathing," I teased.

"Guilty!" he said.

As if she heard, Myra's mother popped into the den. "It's time to eat."

Myra's dad joined us and said, "We have quite the crew here. The star quarterback, captain of the color guard, two tennis champions, and our soon-to-be valedictorian."

"Don't jinx me, Dad," Myra said.

"Can we have a blessing before we eat?" Myra's dad asked. Without waiting, he continued, "Dear God, thank you for these wonderful young people gathered in our home, for this time we have to share, and for this food you have provided. Amen."

After we ate, we took Sandra home. Will gave her a long kiss, then hopped back into the car. When we stopped in our driveway, Will hurried out of the car. "I'll give you two a moment," he said then went into the house.

We stopped at the door. "Thanks for going with me tonight. It was great," Ben said.

"I had a good time, too." *I wonder if he's going to kiss me this time.* He didn't wait and pulled me in for a kiss. *Definitely no sparks.*

When I felt his tongue push into my mouth, I pulled back. *Ick!* I couldn't help it. "Thanks for a nice evening." *I wanted him to get the idea it was over.*

"Yeah. Maybe we can go out again sometime."

"Sure." He seemed lost for a moment, then walked to his car.

"Good night," he called back.

"Good night."

I just stood there as he drove off. Every nerve in my body was zinging. *I should have liked that. It wasn't that bad. But no. No. I wasn't ready for the tongue. That was too much. I feel so conflicted! Ben is nice, but there is no chemistry. At least I wasn't repulsed. I wasn't. I don't think. Was I? Why else would I have pulled away? Ugh! This is so hard! It shouldn't be so hard!*

I'm not sure how long I stood there. The sound of the door opening brought me back. Will poked his head out and saw that Ben was gone. "You coming in?"

"Yeah. I was just thinking."

As soon as I closed the door, he asked, "Well?"

I knew what he meant but asked, "Well what?" anyway.

"You know, how was it?"

"Weird."

"What do you mean, weird?"

"I don't feel like I thought I would."

"Well, how do you feel?"

"Conflicted."

"Weird."

"Ben seems to be a nice guy, but I feel… I guess I don't really feel anything. I wasn't repulsed when he kissed me, I don't think, but there sure weren't any fireworks."

"Interesting. I'm going to bed. You know the parentals will be waking us up for church."

It was 2:27 when I lay down. Taz hopped onto the bed and went through her kneading ritual before lying down next to me. I rolled onto my side and into my thoughts. Feelings and thoughts and sleep battled. Sleep finally won.

Chapter 5

Sunday, October 21, 2018

My sleep had been fitful, and I awoke tired. Dreams kept waking me up. Taz rubbed against my shoulder. I looked at the clock: 11:15.

It hit me that it was Sunday, and in a panic I flew out of bed, prompting an accusatory meow from Taz. I hurried into the kitchen and then down the hall to Will's room. No one was home. *Why didn't they wake me up?*

I walked back to the kitchen to find Taz busy at her food dish. The sight triggered my hunger. I had some juice and a bowl of cereal.

After breakfast, I pulled out my diary to try to process my current state.

Today started out weirdly. My family left me behind for church. I assume they couldn't wake me up. I had a date last night with Ben. We went to the homecoming dance then to Myra's for breakfast. He kissed me at the end.

I'm still not sure what I think about it. He's a nice guy, but when he tried to French kiss me, I pulled away. It was awful! I'm not sure why. Maybe he is just not the right guy.

Anyway, I think my crisis is over. I know I can be straight. That will be a relief to my family and friends. I just hope my heart comes along.

I pulled into the church parking lot just behind Myra. It was time for youth group. She came running and grabbed me in a hug.

"Are you OK? I was worried when you didn't make it to church!"

"I'm fine. I don't know why they didn't wake me up."

"Will said they tried, but you just kept grunting and going back to sleep. Are you sure you're not sick?"

"I must have just been tired. It was a short night, and I didn't sleep much. I kept having dreams and waking up."

"What were they about?"

"I can't remember, but I think they were stressful, like when you dream you're falling off a cliff and wake up just before you die."

"Lovely!"

"Wait, I just remembered one. People were lined up for a game of tug of war. They started pulling, and I was cheering them on. Then all of a sudden, I was the rope, and they were pulling me by the arms and feet. It hurt so bad, and I thought they were going to pull me in half." I was tensing up just talking about it.

"I'm glad you woke up before that happened! What a stressful night! So what did you think of Ben? Inquiring minds need to know."

"It was great. I have decided that I'm straight after all."

"Did he kiss you?" Myra asked with a grin.

"He did."

"Was it wonderful?"

"Well, no."

"I see."

"What do you mean, 'I see?'"

"It sounds like it left you cold."

"I'm sure he's just not the right guy. I'll have to keep looking."

"Girl, you have a long way to go to figure you out. I think you're living that nightmare. Let's go in."

Myra's words stuck in my heart as we walked to the youth room. *No, she's wrong. I have it figured out. Maybe she is speaking wisdom. Maybe I'm trying to force myself to be something I'm not. No. I'm straight. Ugh! I am living that nightmare!*

Roger was leading the first song when we sat down. Will waved from across the room where he sat next to Sandra. I waved back, then my blood froze. Ben was sitting right behind Will. The pull of the nightmare got stronger.

"What's Ben doing here?" I whispered to Myra.

"Silly girl! Why do you think he's here."

"Did you invite him?"

"That may be a possibility."

"Ugh!"

When Roger had us stand for the last song before the lesson, Ben worked his way over to me. "Hey."

"Hey, Ben."

"I like your church. It's nice."

"Thanks."

He sat down next to me. I tried not to show my consternation. I kept my eyes on Roger, feigning interest in the lesson. My feelings were whipping my thoughts into a whirlwind, so I had no idea what Roger was talking about.

This is crazy! I should be happy that he is here. I should want to hold his hand. I should be looking forward to the lesson ending so I can talk to him. But what I should be, I'm not. I just can't deal with this right now. I think I'm losing my mind!

Roger finally finished the lesson. After the song and closing prayer, Ben said, "I could go for more Bellini's gelato. Would you like some?"

"No!" I snapped. I saw the hope drain from his face. *Ugh! I don't want to hurt him. I have to do this.*

I grabbed his hand and dragged him out of the room and down the hall where we could talk privately.

"Ben, I have to be honest with you." I could see the tension building on his face. "I don't want to hurt you, but I'm just not able to be in a relationship right now."

I expected that to be the end of that and he would just walk away.

"Oh," he said. "But I like you a lot."

Great! This isn't going to be as easy as I'd hoped.

"I like you, too. You're a nice guy."

"I don't see the problem then. Let's just take it slow and go out some. I'm not asking you to marry me."

OK. He deserves to know the truth. I'm tired of lying. Here goes.

"Let me be totally honest, but I need you to promise to keep this to yourself. I'm not ready for everyone to know."

"OK. What is it?"

"I'm not sure that I'm straight. I'm trying to figure me out."

"Oh."

"Please don't tell anyone. I'll just die if this gets out, but I thought I owed you an honest explanation."

"I don't understand."

What is there not to understand?

"Let me put it this way. I think I'm lesbian."

"But you kissed me."

"I know. I don't know what's going on right now. I thought if I went out with you, I could prove to myself that I'm straight. Now I'm just more confused. Can't you see that I'm a hot mess?"

"I see. Well, do you want to go for gelato?"

"Ugh!" I had nothing left to say. I turned and walked off, leaving Ben standing there. I didn't look back.

"Girl, you're stomping so hard you're shaking the whole church!" Myra said. "What's up?"

"I told Ben the truth."

"You didn't! The whole truth?"

"Yep. I felt like he deserved to know."

"That may come back to haunt you."

Chapter 6

Wednesday, October 31, 2018

As we were walking out the door, Mom called, "Don't forget the candy!"

"Got it, Mom!" we said at the same time.

It was 4:30pm, and Trunk or Treat started at 5:30.

"We'll have to decorate in a hurry!" Will said.

"You go on and get started. I have a mission to do first."

"I thought you were riding with me. What are you going to do? I need help decorating the car."

"I'm going to drop some candy by Witchaleea's."

"On Halloween? You're brave! Hurry! Don't let her cut out your eye for her witch's brew."

"Good grief! Give her a break."

"OK, Saint Willow. See you at the church. But hurry!"

The sky sported marvelous shades of pink as I pulled into Witchaleea's driveway. I admired the sunset for a minute, then picked up the small bag of candy and marched to the door.

When I opened the screen to knock, the door flew open. I was so startled, I nearly lost my balance on the step.

"Hi! I brought you some candy."

"You have taken a step forward. Good for you. It is a hard climb, though… Candy!"

A step forward? Does she want me to come in? I decided to talk instead. "My name's Willow. What is yours?" I tried again with an introduction.

"Yes, names are important. Willows drink deeply."

"I see. Would you mind telling me your name?" I prompted.

"Grace." The door closed, and she was gone.

I stood there puzzling again over this odd lady. Just as I closed the screen, the door popped open again. "Thank you for the candy. You are a kind soul."

"You're welcome," I said to the closing door. *Well, OK then. I have to get to the church to help Will decorate the car!*

I resisted the urge to press the accelerator harder than necessary while I thought about Grace's comments. *Grace is definitely better than Witchaleea! What did she mean by, "You have taken a step forward?" Was she talking about me almost falling off her step? Was I standing closer than the last time? Maybe that's it! Last time I was standing on the carport rather than the step. Still, she is an odd bird.*

I saw Will attaching what would be the top row of dragon teeth and hurried over to help.

"It's looking good!"

"Perfect timing! I'm not sure I can get these teeth on by myself, and I know I can't do the head without help." He stopped and looked me over. "I see you escaped without the loss of any body parts!"

"Good grief, Will! She's not a witch! She is odd, though."

We worked together to get the dragon's head strapped on, then turned on the compressor to blow it up. I stood back, making sure it was straight while Will arranged a string of red lights in the back of the trunk.

John and Wyatt from the youth group walked by. "I didn't know they let dykes do Trunk or Treat," John said just loudly enough for me to hear. Wyatt laughed, and they kept walking.

A mixture of anger and hurt froze me in place. Will pulled his head out of the trunk and admired his work. "It looks just like you're reaching into a dragon's..." He stopped when he saw me. "What's wrong?" He looked back at the car. "I think it looks great."

"John just called me a dyke." I gestured with my chin in the direction he was walking. That was the only part of my body I seemed to be able to move.

"They're creeps, anyway. They may have been talking about me. Who knows?"

"Why would they do that?" I wondered out loud. Then it hit me. "Ben! I bet Ben told them. I'm going to kill him when I see him!"

"Why would Ben do that? How could Ben do that? Does he know? Did you tell him?"

"I did. I felt I had to. I told him that day he came to youth group. He was trying to start a relationship, and I couldn't handle it. I thought I owed him the truth. I see I was wrong!" The anger freed my body, and I was able to move in a jittery pace, back and forth.

"Still, they may have just been being their usual jerky selves."

A hot tear slithered out of my eye. "I have to pull myself together. We have to be happy and create some fun for the kids."

Myra and Jaynie came hustling over. "We're all set up. Do you need any help?" Myra asked.

"All we have left is the bottom dentures," Will said. "This should be fun."

"Yeah, it's always fun to see the kiddos all excited," Myra added.

"Willow, the word is going around that you're gay. I told them it's not true," Jaynie said. She had a serious expression.

I cringed. *He is spreading the word everywhere!* "I'm sure I have Ben to thank for that. It may or may not be true. I'm still trying to figure it out. Please don't spread any rumors! I'm at my wits end with all of this!"

"Oh!" Jaynie said. Her mouth was opened so wide I could see her uvula. "I just can't believe it! You seem so normal!"

"I don't feel normal right now. I'm lost in the woods and there are fifty trails to follow. I can't figure out which is the right one."

The next thing I knew, I was in Myra's arms. "We're here for you. You're not in those woods alone."

"Thanks. You're the best!" I hugged her back.

"The dragon is ready to eat kiddos for dinner!" Will said lowering and raising the hatchback like it was chewing. "Time to put on our show faces and have some fun."

I knew he was telling me to suck it up and get ready for the kids. The first car pulled up, and five children hopped out.

"Don't be terrorizing these kids!" Myra said as she and Jaynie hustled back to Myra's car.

"I hate to see this guy go. He was quite the hit!" Will said after the last child had come through.

"We should save him for next year."

While I was removing the lights, these nasty words floated into the trunk: "There she is again. Don't walk too close!"

It was Wyatt this time. I bumped my head as I jerked it out of the car. Before I could say anything, I heard Will. "Guys, this is *supposed* to be a Christian activity. You know, love one another as Jesus loved us. Try to grow up!"

They just sniggered and walked on.

Back home, curled up in the bed with Taz purring beside me, I tried to process the day by writing in my diary.

I may have had the first taste of my new life tonight. A couple of jerks called me a dyke. I guess they are right. I know now. I guess I may have always known. It's just hard to admit it to myself since everybody is so against gay people. I have always been told it's wrong. I apparently believed it enough to stuff it down and hide it even from myself. It seems funny how softly and easily my acceptance came today.

I stopped and scratched the back of Taz's neck. *At least Taz still loves me.* She stood, stretched, and rubbed her chin on mine. I resumed writing.

Being called a dyke wasn't the bad part. They are just pricks. The hurtful part was they said I shouldn't be part of a church activity. That can't be right. If God loves me enough for Jesus to die for me, why wouldn't God want me in church? It will be devastating if I'm kicked out of the church. I won't know what to do. Well, I just won't let that happen. They will have to accept me for who I am. First, I guess, I have to accept me for who I am. OK, from now on, I am Willow, and I am lesbian. Let the chips fall where they will. I refuse to pretend to be someone I'm not any longer. Tomorrow is a new day!

Chapter 7

Thursday, November 1, 2018

The eastern sky was fired with glorious shades of pink as I drove to school. It brought warmth to the chilly morning. I felt a tap on my back as I leaned in for my backpack.

"Good morning!" Myra chirped. "How are you?"

"I'm good. How about you?"

"I was worried about you after last night."

"Last night was quite a night. Something about John calling me a dyke made me realize that I am gay. I think I have always known that but just kept it stuffed down inside. The biggest problem has been admitting it to myself. I did that last night, and I feel a deep peace today."

"Good."

"Good?"

"Yeah. Now you can quit torturing yourself and get back to living!"

"It has been a rough couple of weeks, but today is the first day of my new life!"

"Great! Let's start it with some AP calculus!"

On the way to class, I saw John and Wyatt walking our way. I grabbed my backpack straps and squeezed.

"Is the queer still here?" John called as he passed.

"Shut up, John!" Myra responded. She grabbed my arm. "Come on before you do something you'll regret."

"Who is that?" I whispered to Myra as we sat down.

"It looks like we have a new student."

"She has a radical hairdo!" I said, eyeing her spiky blond hair with its green highlights.

The tardy bell rang, and Mr. Carlisle said, "Good morning. I trust everyone had a horror-filled Halloween! I'm sure you've noticed that we have a new student with us this morning. I'm happy to welcome Liia Nyberg to our class. She is from Sweden. Her mom was transferred here as an engineer, and her dad is an author who is quite well known in Sweden. Everybody say, 'Hey,' to Liia."

We all responded with, "Hey, Liia!"

"We won't go around and have everyone say their names, because I don't believe there is any way she could remember them anyway. But please introduce yourselves after class. Today we are set to begin second differentials. While the first differential gives us the rate of change of the equation, the second one gives us the rate of change of the change: the acceleration."

I glanced to my right and could see Liia's profile. A bright green eye over a delicate nose was quite a contrast to her wild hair. *It will be fun having a foreign student in our class. I've never known anyone from Sweden. Uh-oh! I haven't been paying attention!* I tried to tune back in to the lesson.

After class, Myra grabbed my arm again. "Come on! Let's introduce ourselves!" We hustled over to Liia.

"Hi, I'm Myra. Welcome to Hawksville!"

"And I'm Willow. It's nice to meet you. I've never known anyone from Sweden."

Thanks! It is nice to meet you," she said.

I love her accent!

"We're happy to help if you need anything," Myra offered.

"I could use help finding my next class. It's physics."

"That's where I'm going! You can walk with me." I said.

"I'm off to chemistry. It was nice to meet you!

"Myra plans to go into pharmaceutical research and find a cure for cancer."

"Wow! That's ambitious."

There was a break after second period, so I invited Liia to hang out with Myra, Jaynie, and me. We met in our usual spot just outside the B hall.

"Hey, Jaynie! You have to meet Liia! She's a new student, and she's from Sweden," I said as we walked up.

"Hi, Liia. Nice to meet you," Jaynie said. "I bet it's cold in Sweden."

"Ja, we get snow this time of year," she answered.

"We will probably get three or four snows this winter, but not much," I explained.

"That's nice. Snow gets tiresome," Liia said.

"No way! I love snow!" Myra said.

"They cancel school here when it snows," Jaynie pointed out.

Something didn't feel right, and I looked around. Ben and a couple of his friends were walking by. I clenched my teeth.

"I know that look. It spells trouble," Myra said.

I stomped off after Ben. "Hey! I need to talk to you!"

One of his friends punched him in the arm. "Ooooh! Now you're in for it! We'll wait to see if you survive."

"What do you think you're doing telling people that I'm lesbian? I asked you not to tell anyone, but no! You go and tell the whole school!"

"I'm sorry…"

I cut him off. "You're sorry? Now you have people running around calling me dyke. I don't appreciate that at all."

"Willow, my friends wanted to know why we weren't seeing each other anymore. I had to tell them the truth. And I asked them not to say anything. I guess they couldn't keep their mouths shut." He looked over at his friends. Both had smirks on their faces.

"I see you and your friends are having a good time at my expense! Just so you know, if I were straight, I would never want to go out with you again!" I stomped back to Myra, Jaynie, and Liia, not looking back.

"What was that all about? It looked like you were chewing him out." Myra said.

"I'll tell you later." I tried to calm down.

I met up with Myra by our lockers after school.

"You have some explaining to do, girlfriend," Myra said.

"Wait till we get outside." We walked in silence to Myra's car. Her green Leaf was parked a dozen spaces closer to the school than my Jeep.

"OK, spill the beans. What did Ben do to deserve such a thrashing?"

"I guess I kind of lost it and went all ape on him, didn't I?"

"Maybe just a little."

"I'm sure it was him who told people that I'm lesbian. Since he got the whole 'dyke' thing going, I thought he deserved to know how I felt about it."

"I see. Do you feel better now?"

"Not really. No."

"Willow, you can't let your emotions get knocked out of joint every time someone calls you a name. Unfortunately, there is probably a lot more of that to come."

"I know, but that's easier said than done."

"You've got that right."

I paused and looked at the cotton ball clouds. "I'm scared. I see how other gay folks get treated, and I'm not looking forward to that."

"Yeah, but you're different."

"How so?"

"You've got me on your side." She laid her backpack in the back seat and gave me a hug.

"Thanks. I think I'm going to need you."

"You know I'll be here for you."

"I do. I couldn't ask for a better friend. OK, I'm off to meet Will at the tennis court. We have to get in all the practice we can if we're going to win state."

"If anyone can win it, it's you!"

I drove to the court with my mind spinning faster than the tires. *Myra's right. I have to brace myself for the taunts and go on with my life. I wonder what my life will be like now. Will I find someone to be with? Oh God, what will my parents think?*

"Hey, Sis," Will called from the court where he was already hitting serves. Whack! It landed right in the outside corner of the service box.

"Wicked!" I pulled my racket from the back seat and hustled to the court.

"So are you still lesbian or back to straight?"

"Will!"

"Just checking. It has changed a lot lately."

"Don't tease me, please. I'm having a hard enough time as it is."

"OK. I'll try to resist. Hey, did you see the new Swedish girl at school?"

"Yeah, she's in my math and physics classes."

"She's hot!"

"You'd better not let Sandra hear you say that!"

He looked around, pretending he was looking for her. "I think I'm safe. What made you decide for sure that you're into girls?"

I paused, trying to find a way to explain. "Do you know how you feel when you see a hot girl? How your eyes automatically follow her?"

"You mean you've noticed?"

"That's how I feel, too."

"So you think the new girl is hot?"

"Her name is Liia. And yes, I think she's quite the looker. Now let me beat you at some tennis."

"In your dreams!"

Chapter 8

Friday, November 2, 2018

I awoke with a start, jumping and scaring Taz off the bed. The dream was so vivid I felt like it was still happening. I shook my head to try to come out of it. Taz hopped back up and rubbed against me.

"I had an awful dream," I told her.

"Meow."

"I was in a dark, spooky mansion, and I could hear doors creaking way off. But the sounds kept getting closer. I knew somebody or something was coming, and it was after me. I ran up one flight of stairs, and it kept coming. I ran up another flight and found a wardrobe. I climbed in and hid." Taz seemed to be paying attention.

"Then I heard the door open. The floor creaked as footsteps crossed the room. I screamed when the door opened. That's when I woke up."

Taz nuzzled me with her chin.

"You're such a good listener." As I hugged her to me, the alarm sounded. I jumped, causing Taz to jump to the other side of the bed. I crossed the room and shut off the annoying sound. I keep the alarm over there so I have to get up to turn it off. It prevents me from just cutting it off and going back to sleep.

"Ok, I'm up," I said to myself. I squinted at the assault of the light and searched my closet. *What does a queer person wear? Do I need to change my style?*

Taz meowed and curled up on the pile of covers.

"So you think that's a boring idea, huh? I guess you're right. I haven't really changed. I'm still me." I pulled out my favorite Friday jeans and a light sweater and dressed.

"Taz, move so I can make the bed." She stretched out her paw. "OK, I'm starting." I pulled the covers, and Taz stayed put, just sliding along. "Silly cat." Finally she stood, stretched and hopped off the bed. At ten years old, she didn't move as quickly as she used to.

"I'm glad you didn't feel the need to hurry." As soon as I finished, she hopped back up for another nap.

I headed to the bathroom to finish getting ready. Will popped out of his room with his backpack on one shoulder. "You'd better hurry!"

"I'll get there. Don't worry." I wanted to tell him about my dream, but there wasn't time. *That will have to wait.* I glanced at my watch. *Uh-oh!* My confidence about making it to school on time was cracked. I finished getting ready in a frenzy and hustled to class, maybe speeding just a bit.

My front foot made it through the classroom door just as the tardy bell rang. *Technically I made it!* I was jittery from rushing to get there. My hands shook when I opened my notebook. My mind kept going back to the dream, and I just couldn't shake the feeling that someone was after me.

Liia leaned over and whispered, "Good morning! You cut that close!"

"Yeah, I made it by the skin of my teeth." I saw confusion wash over her face. "I'll explain later." I looked over and smiled at Myra.

When calculus was over, I touched Liia on the shoulder. "Do you want to hang out with us again at break?"

"I'd love to, but you will have to explain the skin on your teeth."

Myra and I laughed. "It's just a saying. It means a really close call."

"I have a lot to learn about Americanisms!"

When we met back up at break, I told them about my dream. "It's still spooking me. I just can't get it out of my head."

After a minute, Myra pulled me aside and spoke lowly. "I find it interesting that you were hiding in a closet. Instead of coming to get you, could they have been coming to help you 'come out of the closet' as the saying goes?"

"Wow!" The tone of the whole dream shifted in my spirit and warmth spread in my chest, emerging as a smile.

"I think you're right. I've been addled all morning, but now I'm happy! Thanks, Myra! You're a genius!"

"What was that about?" Jaynie asked when we rejoined the group.

"Secrets are secret," Myra said with a grin.

After school, I was craving sugar. When I met Myra at the lockers I asked, "Do you want to hit Bellini's for a sugar rush? I'll drive."

"Sure, but it'll have to be quick. I have a paper due in three days."

"You're always so diligent. OK, I'll eat fast, even if I get a brain freeze."

When we stepped out the door, I saw Liia ahead on the sidewalk. "Should we invite Liia?"

"Good idea! It must be hard starting off in a new country. At least she speaks English. Hey, Liia. Wait up!"

We caught up and invited her to go with us.

"I'd love to, but I'll have to check with my dad first. He's probably already on his way to pick me up."

"Hurry and call him," Myra said. "Let's walk to the car while you talk. It will save time."

"Myra's very efficient," I explained. On our way to the parking lot, I saw Grace sitting in the carport wearing a long wool coat. I waved, and she returned a slow wave.

"Wow! That's amazing! You got Witchaleea to wave," Myra said.

"I've taken her some goodies a couple of times. Her real name is Grace."

"You actually went over there! Did you see a dead body inside?" Myra asked.

"I haven't been inside, but I'm sure there is no dead body," I scolded.

"What are you talking about?" Liia asked.

"See the old woman in the carport?" Myra said. "There have been rumors going around forever that she is an old witch. People even say she killed her roommate and kept the body in the house."

"That's spooky," Liia said. "Ridiculous, but spooky."

When we got to the parking lot, Myra looked at her watch. "OK, I'm going to drive and meet y'all there. It'll save a few minutes."

"Wow! I've heard the word y'all exists, but that's the first time I've ever heard it spoken," Liia said.

"You might as well get used to it," Myra said.

"Dad actually asked if I'm sure you, y'all, are OK to be with! Good grief!"

"Let's send him a picture so he can see just how evil we look!" I offered.

Liia snapped a photo of the three of us and sent it. "I can text him when I'm ready to be picked up. I feel bad because he was almost here."

"He's probably happy you're making friends," I said. "When we get to Bellini's you can text him that I'll be happy to drive you home."

"You're right. He wants me to make friends. He'll be happy with that, not that he would mind picking me up. He's very supportive."

"That's good to hear." I cranked the Jeep and wondered, *Will my parents be supportive when they find out who I really am? I'm not going to dwell on that right now. I have a new friend to get to know!*

I held the door open for Liia. "I hope you're good at decisions because they have a lot of flavors!"

"What do you like to do for fun?" Liia asked after having ordered a dulce de leche.

"The usual for you?" Lacey, the regular worker, asked me.

"Of course. Dark chocolate cherry is the best!" I turned to Liia. "Will, my brother, and I play tennis. We're hoping to make it to the state championships this spring. How about you?"

"I hate to admit it, but I haven't had much fun since we moved. It's been a hard transition."

"Well that's about to change! You will have to hang out with Myra and me," I said as Myra walked up.

"I see you waited for me," Myra teased.

"I knew you'd be in a hurry, so we just sped up the process."

"Uh huh. Are you sure it wasn't the delicious gelato calling to you?"

"I'll never tell!"

We got our gelatos and sat down. "I like your hair," Myra said to Liia. "The green really brings out your eyes."

"Thanks! So you don't think it's a bit much? I feel it's out of place here."

"The important thing is for you to be you. If people don't like it, that's their problem," Myra said.

"Myra's our local fount of wisdom," I said, and we laughed. "Liia was saying that she has had a hard transition with her move. I told her she will have to start hanging out with us."

"Of course!" Myra said. "We're good for whatever ails you!"

"Thanks! You two, I mean y'all, are kind. I have needed some friends."

"Folks, I have a paper to write, so I'm off. See you tomorrow!" Myra said, picking up her purse and empty gelato cup.

I drove Liia home. "I'm glad you came with us," I said as I parked.

"Yes, that was nice. Have a good afternoon."

I watched her walk to the door. She turned and waved. *I have a new friend!*

Chapter 9

Wednesday, November 14, 2018

I heard a commotion while walking to my locker after school. The sounds of girls hollering grated my ears. *A fight!*

Someone shouted, "This town is no place for queers!" I felt an adrenaline rush as I hurried toward the corner around which the sounds emanated. Fear and anger pierced my heart when I heard the sound of someone crashing into a locker.

Anger won over the fear, and I rushed around the corner. Three girls had another one surrounded and pinned against the locker. I rushed forward and pushed one of the girls aside. "Leave her alone!" I yelled. "I should have known you'd be behind this, Janice!"

"Look, now we have two! Y'all should get together and kiss! How about it, Robin? Don't you want to kiss her? We'd love to watch, wouldn't we?" Janice taunted.

"Maybe we should help them get together," Brenda said.

"I agree," Alexa added.

"Grab them!" Janice ordered. Alexa grabbed Robin from behind and held her by looping her arms through Robin's elbows. Brenda tried to grab me. I elbowed her in the gut, turned, and delivered a kick to her knee. Brenda hit the ground in tears.

Janice shoved me against the lockers before I could turn around. "You don't treat my friend that way!"

I stomped on her instep then shoved her away. She tripped going backward and crashed.

Mr. Carlisle rounded the corner in a trot. "Stop it! Now!" He stopped, straightened his six foot three frame, ran a hand through his salt and pepper hair, and surveyed the situation.

I was about to attack Alexa but held back.

"To the office. Now!" Mr. Carlisle ordered.

"But she started it," Janice lied, pointing to me.

"I very much doubt that," he said. "Now get up and go."

Robin jerked away from Alexa and stomped toward the principal's office. I followed, still feeling in fight mode. Brenda and Janice got up and came behind Alexa.

Mr. Carlisle worked his way around us and knocked on Principal Taylor's door. Robin caught my eye and whispered, "Thank you."

"You're welcome," I whispered back. I could hear Mr. Carlisle explaining to Dr. Taylor what he had found.

"I heard a commotion and found these five girls fighting. They will have to explain the rest."

"Girls, will you please come in?" Dr. Taylor ordered. She stood and looked each of us in the eye. My hands were shaking. Fear returned to mix with my anger. *I've never been sent to the principal's office. I wonder what's going to happen.*

Dr. Taylor sat back down. "Fighting is not allowed in this school. I won't have it! I'm sure each of you will offer a different explanation of what happened."

"We were just talking to Robin when Willow attacked us," Janice butted in.

"Did I ask you to speak?" Dr. Taylor barked and gave Janice a glare that made me cringe.

"That's not true. They were attacking me for being lesbian, and Willow jumped in to save me," Robin explained.

"I don't recall asking you to speak, either," Dr. Taylor said. She paused. "Good. I'm glad you can hold your tongues. Fighting is not allowed here, as I was saying. You will each have in-school suspension for Thursday and Friday. After that, I trust your attitudes will be sufficiently adjusted. Do I make myself clear?"

"Yes, ma'am," I said, my heart and head dropping. Robin echoed me. The other three just stood silently.

"I will be calling each of your parents. Janice, Alexa, and Brenda, you may go. I don't want any more of this foolishness," Dr. Taylor said, giving each a stern look.

I wanted to run. My mind was racing. *Why can't we leave, too? I'm going to die when my parents find out!* I noticed an evil smirk on Janice's face as she turned to leave.

"Thank you, Mr. Carlisle," Dr. Taylor said.

"Have a good afternoon," he said and left, closing the door.

"Sit down, girls." She waited for us to sit. My knees felt stiff as I tried to settle into the chair. "First of all, Robin, I suspect that your version of the story is more accurate. I have known all of you since you started. Willow, I'm surprised you resorted to fighting rather than using your words to calm the situation."

"I tried, but they attacked me, too."

"I see. Here's the thing: If you are going to claim to be gay, you can expect this kind of treatment. Unfortunately, it is just the way people are.

"As part of your 'punishment,'" she said, making air quotes, "I'm going to have you set up some sessions with the counselor. And yes, I've heard the rumors about you two thinking you are lesbian. Maybe she can help you resolve this fancy so you can get back to being normal girls."

Oooh! How dare she say that! I wanted to lash out and struggled to hold my tongue.

She continued. "I realize that homosexuality is all the rage right now, but you will regret taking that path later when you realize you want a traditional life. It's best to stop it now. That's all I have to say on the matter. You may leave."

It dawned on me that I was stomping through the secretary's office, so I tried to walk normally. Out in the hall, I hit my hand on the wall so hard it hurt. "Ouch!"

"Can you believe that woman?" I was in my own little world and jumped when Robin spoke. "I can't believe she thinks the counselor can talk us into being straight," she continued.

I looked at her, trying to process her words. I felt I was down deep in a well again.

"Are you OK?" Robin asked.

Tears welled and spilled over. "No, I'm not OK. My soul is falling to pieces, and I don't know what is going to happen."

"You're strong. You've got this," Robin said.

I wiped the tears and willed myself to calm down. I took three deep breaths. "Thanks, Robin. Why do you not seem as devastated as I do?"

"I've been at this a long time. There are a bunch of people that act like goats. You learn to let it just run off your back and carry on."

"Thanks. I hope I can learn that. We've never really been friends. I hope that will change."

"I think we can make that happen," Robin said with a smile.

"Now I guess we have to face the music at home."

Driving home I tried to find the right words to explain this to my parents. Then it hit me. *What if Dr. Taylor tells them I'm lesbian? What am I going to do?* I was so shocked I ran off the road but recovered before I hit the ditch.

My nerves were zinging when I pulled into the driveway. Will had just gotten out of his Prius. I took another three deep breaths to collect myself.

"I see you had a rough day," he said.

I love the way that we can read each other so easily. "Yeah, I got into a fight and will have in-school suspension for two days."

"You got into a fight? I can't believe it!"

"Hold your voice down," I whispered. "Janice and her cronies were attacking Robin. When I tried to stop them, they attacked me, too."

"Mom and Dad will hit the ceiling! Maybe they'll go easy on you since it's your first offense."

"Yeah, right. She's also making me see the counselor to try to fix my gayness."

"That's just not right. Anyway, I recommend a preemptive strike. It would be better for them to hear it from you than from Dr. Taylor."

"You're right. I hope she hasn't called yet. Mom did have to work from home today."

"Time to face the music."

I walked in and could hear music coming from the office. "Hey, Mom. We're home."

Mom popped out of the office dressed in a nice blouse, sweat pants, and slippers.

"Nice outfit," Will teased.

"Thanks! So how was the day?"

"Mine was typical," Will said.

"You look stressed, Willow."

"Yeah, we need to talk."

"Oh. OK."

Will went on to his room.

"What is it?" Mom asked, sitting down at the kitchen table.

I sat down, too, nerves jittering.

"I got into a fight at school today." *Might as well just lay it out there!*

"I see. Tell me what happened."

"So Dr. Taylor hasn't called yet?"

"No."

"I happened on three bullies picking on a girl. They had her pinned against a locker. I tried to get them to stop, but they attacked me, too. I defended myself." *I decided to leave out the part about us being lesbians.*

"It sounds to me like you did the right thing. But I guess you are in trouble anyway."

"In-school suspension. Dr. Taylor didn't even want to know what happened. She just punished all of us… even Robin, who was doing nothing wrong."

"The school policy is that anyone involved in a fight gets punished. I think they figured out it is too hard to learn the truth when you have two parties with different stories."

"You don't seem mad."

"I'm actually proud of you for sticking up for someone being bullied."

"Thanks. I won the fight, by the way," I said with a grin. "That self-defense class came in handy."

"How long will your in-school suspension be?"

"Tomorrow and Friday."

"Just remember that you were in the right and take the punishment. It will go away soon."

"Thanks, Mom."

Will apparently heard my door close. He popped in three seconds later. "Well?"

"She wasn't even mad! She even said she was proud of me for standing up to bullies."

"You didn't tell her the rest, then."

"No, and I hope Dr. Taylor doesn't."

Chapter 10

Thursday, November 15, 2018

I was a bit rattled as I walked into the in-school suspension room. There were a dozen other students sitting silently. Robin looked up with a sad face. Janice leered at me. A big sign read, "No Talking." The teachers rotated monitoring the room during their free periods. The first period monitor was Ms. Quiros, my Spanish teacher. She nodded and pointed to an empty desk.

I sat down and was surprised to find a list of my assignments for the day already on the desk. *I guess this means all my teachers know what happened.* My cheeks flushed.

Not ever having done this before, I didn't know the routine. I held up the list of assignments and looked to Ms. Quiros. She nodded again. I started the calculus assignment.

At 9:45am the door opened. Everyone looked up to see the counselor, Shirley Simpson, standing there. She caught my eye and motioned for me to come.

My heart galloped. My cheeks flushed again. I hurried out of the room as quickly as I could.

Ms. Simpson sat down in an armchair and gestured for me to sit on the couch. *I guess this is where I start my lesbian cessation lessons.* My nerves were taut. I sat and waited. Ms. Simpson pushed back her jet black hair and adjusted her large, black-framed glasses.

I looked into her bright blue eyes and sensed a caring soul was looking back. I relaxed just a bit. *Maybe she will be easy to talk to.*

"Willow, I assume you know why you are here. Dr. Taylor wants me to talk with you about your homosexuality. Are you homosexual?"

"Yes, ma'am." *I decided not to try to hide it from her.*

"It is my understanding that this is a new thing for you."

"Yes, ma'am."

"How do you feel about it?"

"Scared."

"Why scared?"

"Because I want to fit in. I'm afraid of what my parents will think when they find out. It's all so new, and I don't know what to do." The words just poured out.

"First off, I want you to know that I think homosexuality is something a person is born with, not a choice one makes. OK, we have gotten talking about your sexual orientation out of the way. What I really want to talk with you about is the fight."

I was stunned. Time stopped as I tried to process what I had just heard. "But I thought you were supposed to be telling me that being homosexual is wrong and that I need to be straight."

"So did Dr. Taylor," Ms. Simpson said with a laugh. "She is of the opinion that homosexuality is something people choose, like jumping on the latest fad. But I don't believe that, and I don't want you to think that, either."

"I don't know what to say."

"Tell me about the fight. What happened?"

I told her everything that happened, including how I fought off Brenda and Janice.

"Why did you intervene? You could have just called for a teacher."

Interesting. I hadn't thought about that before. "I was angry. They were attacking her just because she is different from them. I didn't mean to fight. I pushed Alexa away and told them to leave Robin alone. I thought that would be enough, but then they started trying to force us to kiss."

"I see. How did it feel when they turned on you?"

"Bad."

"Tell me more about how you felt in the moment they attacked you."

She is easy to talk to. I think I can trust her with the truth. I pushed on, taking the chance. "I think I felt like I was being raped. They were trying to force me to do something I didn't want to do. I was afraid and angry all at the same time. I remembered the moves I had learned in a self-defense class and fought back. There was no way they were going to beat me."

Ms. Simpson put her hand on my forearm. "I'm sorry you had to go through this, but I'm glad you were there to help Robin. We'll talk again tomorrow."

Walking back to the suspension room, warmth radiated from my heart and generated a smile. *I was expecting a fight but found support. I don't feel so... alone now.*

I walked a little farther then chuckled. *I bet that's not what Dr. Taylor had in mind when she set it up for me to talk with Ms. Simpson.*

The bell to end the day finally rang. I gathered my stuff in my pack, still glowing from my talk with Ms. Simpson. Just outside the door I got knocked off balance by a bump on my shoulder. It was Janice.

"I love you, too!" I called to her back as she stomped away.

"My favorite jailbird is free!" Myra called as I walked up to her just outside the building.

"Funny."

"How was it?"

"Boring. I just had to sit there and do work, but I guess that is how punishment is supposed to be."

"Did you have to talk to Ms. Simpson?"

"Yeah, that was the best part of the day. She was nice and supportive."

"So she didn't set you straight, so to speak?"

"Not at all. She said she thinks homosexuality is something we are born with and that it is OK."

"Good for her."

"I felt a lot better after talking to her."

"Hey, Willow! Are you OK?" I turned and saw Liia hurrying over.

"It was a boring day, but I survived, thanks."

"I heard about the fight and how you got in trouble. In Sweden, it would have been the bullies that got punished, not you. That's just not right."

"Welcome to America," Myra said. "Liberty, justice, and punishment for all."

Thursday, November 22, 2018

It was Thanksgiving morning. I peeked out my window to see a cold drizzle wetting the world. *I'm not getting up yet!* I hopped back in bed with Taz and snuggled under the covers. I was comfortable, but no longer sleepy. I decided to write in my diary.

It's Thanksgiving, 2018. I am a different person this year. I'm beginning to get used to my new skin. But I still dread telling my parents. I can't imagine they will take it well. I don't want to disappoint them, but I have to be true to myself. I can't live a lie just to make them happy.

Will poked his head in. "Happy Thanksgiving!" He came in and shut the door. "So when are you going to tell Mom and Dad your little secret?"

"Well definitely not on Thanksgiving. I don't want to ruin today for them."

"That's kind of you, but you have to tell them sometime."

"I know. That's going to be so hard."

"I'll be there with you, if you'd like me to."

"Thanks. It looks like tennis is off for today."

"Yeah, I checked the weather. It's supposed to rain till late afternoon. By then I'll be too stuffed to play."

"Hey, do you want to come with me to take Grace a plate after we eat?"

"Who's Grace?"

"Alias Witchaleea."

"No, thanks. That would be too scary!"

"Chicken! Really, Will, she's not a witch. She's odd but mostly I think she's just all alone."

"Could you smell the roommate's decaying body when she opened the door?"

"I'm sure the smell is gone by now, don't you think?"

"Really?" *He looked like he believed me.*

"Good grief! You're right, you don't need to come."

After dinner, I got four paper plates from the cabinet. "Mom, I'm going to take a plate to an old woman who lives by herself. Is that OK with you?"

"Sure, Honey. That's kind of you to remember her."

I loaded two plates, covered them with the other two, and sealed them with rubber bands. I drove in the drizzle and parked in Grace's driveway. The door opened before I got to it.

"Willow comes on Thanksgiving. Plates! You have a good heart."

"I brought you food from our table."

Her bony hands reached out and took the plates eagerly. "I will enjoy. Turkey and dressing? I haven't had that since Joy died."

"I heard that your roommate died a while back. I'm sorry."

"She was very special. She's in the bedroom. I would like for you to see her."

I was stunned. Memories of Will's far-fetched tale banged in my head. Grace was waiting. I could see she wanted me to come in.

"I-I-I I'd love to," I finally managed.

"Come." She turned and moved with a speed that surprised me. I hurried to catch up. I followed her down a dark hall. She paused at a closed door before opening it. I was holding my breath.

"Well come on in." My feet hadn't moved. I went in and followed Grace's gaze to the top of a chest of drawers.

An elaborate urn with a raised ivy design sat amidst votive and scented candles. Grace lit the candles.

"I love to sit and look at her in the candlelight," she said.

I breathed again. "It's beautiful," I said once the candles were lit. I blinked back a tear. "She must have been important to you."

"Joy was my very life. I loved her so much." She blew out the candles. "I'm sure you're not interested in hearing of an old woman's sorrows. You must go."

Is she demanding that I leave or saying that she's sure I don't want to stay anymore. I started to tell her I'm not in a hurry when she gestured for me to move into the hall. She shut the door behind us.

I followed her to the kitchen. She held the door for me, and as I stepped out she said, "Willows are good in storms. They can resist the wind." She shut the door.

OK. That was interesting. I walked toward my car and heard the door open again. "Thank you," she called.

"You are so welcome," I said as the door closed.

"How did it go?" Mom asked as I walked into the kitchen. She was still cleaning up.

"She was grateful. I feel sorry for her. She lives all alone."

"Who is she?"

"It's Witchaleea," Will said in a spooky voice.

"The lady that lives near the school?" Mom asked.

"Yes, and her name is Grace.

"You did a good thing, Willow. And Will, you need to show some respect for this lady."

Taz rubbed against my leg and meowed, looking up expectantly. I tore off a piece of turkey, held it up, and said, "Sit up." She sat up on her hind legs, and I gave her the turkey. She purred while she ate, which made me happy.

Walking down the hall, I pulled Will into my room. "Guess what!"

"I give. Tell me."

"Grace invited me in to see her roommate."

"Is she just bones now?"

"She keeps her in the bedroom, just like you said."

"You're kidding me!"

"Nope. She's in an urn on the chest. She has candles all around it."

"I can't believe you actually went in there! You'd better not let our parents find out. They'll put *you* in an urn!"

"Every time I see her she says strange things about my name."

"Like what?"

"This time she said, 'Willows are good in storms.'"

"I hope she's not seeing the future."

Chapter 11

We left the tennis court and hustled to youth group, arriving fifteen minutes late. Roger was already into the lesson.

"Glad you could join us," he sniggered.

I looked around, and there were only about ten of us here. "I knew he should have cancelled today," I whispered to Will as we sat down next to Jaynie.

Roger gave me the "Quiet, please" look, then continued with the lesson.

"Romans eight twenty-nine tells us that we are 'predestined to be conformed to the image' of Jesus. Isn't that a wonderful thought? We can live our lives like Jesus lived his. That means loving our neighbors as Jesus loves us.

"But it also means that we need to help the process along. We can't go about our lives doing things and being things that we know are against Jesus' teachings. If we are to conform to the image of Jesus, we can't lead lifestyles that are out of sync with the Gospel.

"Take a moment to think about your own life. How are you conforming to Christ? What are you doing that doesn't conform? How can you work on the changes? That is your mission this week."

He closed with a prayer. As everyone got up to leave, he walked up and said. "Could I see you and Jaynie in my office for a few minutes?"

In my surprise it took a moment to respond. *I must be in trouble for whispering during the lesson.* I tried a diversion. "Will and I drove together. Could it wait so he doesn't have to sit around waiting on me?"

"That's OK. I'll play a game on my phone," Will said.

I shot him a look that said, "Gee, thanks!"

Following Roger to his office, I mouthed to Jaynie, "What's this about?"

She didn't answer.

Roger unlocked the door and gestured to the love seat in his small office. "Have a seat." He swiveled his desk chair around and sat in it. I sat next to Jaynie and wondered what was coming.

"Let me start by saying that Jaynie is concerned about you," Roger said looking at me. "She told me that you have come out as homosexual but have seemed twisted in knots lately. So how are you doing?"

I cringed and shot Jaynie a look that said, "I'll deal with you later!"

"I'm doing much better now, thank you," I directed to Roger.

"That's good to hear. Does that mean you've decided you are straight?"

"No, I'm definitely homosexual."

He paused, and I watched as the gears turned. "Willow, first of all I want you to know that you are welcome in our youth group no matter what your sexual orientation is. We love you and want you to be a part of this group.

"Secondly, I want you to consider this decision very carefully. It will affect the rest of your life."

"Actually it wasn't a decision. It was more of a discovery. Now I realize I have known all along. I think I stuffed it in the back of my soul so that I would fit in better." I relaxed a bit since he wasn't being judgmental.

"I see. It is important that you feel at home in your own skin, but you need to realize that the homosexual lifestyle goes against the teaching of the church."

I clenched my fist and my heart raced. "So you *were* directing today's lesson at me. I wondered that."

"No, I wasn't directing it at you, but I'm glad you were able to see a call on your life in it."

"If God is a God of love, why wouldn't God love me the way I am? God created me this way, so why not love me?" I stood up as anger made me shake. "I'm leaving."

I stomped down the hall with fire in my veins. I heard footsteps chasing behind me but didn't turn to look.

"Willow, wait!" Jaynie called.

I spun around. "I can't believe you turned me in to him! How dare you!"

"I was just trying to help. I thought you might need to talk to someone. I didn't know he would go all judgmental on you."

"Well you should have known. That's the way he is."

"What's the ruckus?" Will said, coming out the door.

"Jaynie turned me into Roger for being lesbian," I growled.

"I was just trying to help," Jaynie said. "I just want you to be OK. You're my friend."

"And by 'OK,' do you mean straight?" I glared at her.

"I think it's time for me to go. We can talk later," Jaynie said.

I stood ramrod straight with my arms crossed and watched her walk away.

"Um, are you ready to go home?" Will asked.

"I don't want to leave till I'm sure she's gone."

"OK, we'll wait. But I do have homework to get done."

After a minute I said, "Let's go."

On the drive home, Will observed, "You sure are quiet."

"I think everyone is going to reject me."

"Gee thanks."

"Are you sure you're not going to turn on me, too?"

"You know I love you. I'll always be your biggest fan, no matter what."

"Thanks, Will. That means a lot. I wonder if I'm going to have to leave the church."

"No. Why would you think that?"

"Roger started off nice, then turned to how my lifestyle is incompatible with church teaching. I don't know if I can stay where I'm not wanted."

"You're wanted. Everybody there wants you in the church. You can't take Roger too seriously. He's just too black and white. Life requires a little grayness."

I laughed. "Gray is certainly my color right now!"

Chapter 12

On the way into the house, Will hugged me.

"It's going to be OK. Maybe a little rocky to start with, but we'll make it."

"Thanks, Will. You're my favorite brother."

I opened the door, and Mom called from the den. "Willow, we need to talk to you."

I mouthed to Will, "What's up?"

He shrugged.

"OK, let me put up my racket," I answered to give me time to think. I put the racket into the closet and gave Taz a scratch behind her ear before going to the den. *Would Roger have already called?*

"What's up? I asked, noting grave looks on my parents' faces. *I guess he has.*

Mom was seated in the recliner and Dad was standing by the fireplace. "Roger called just before you got home," Mom said.

Oh no!

"He said that you think you are homosexual. Is that true?"

"This is not how I wanted you to find out. I planned to tell you myself. I was trying to get the courage to."

"You mean it's true," Dad growled.

"Yes, it's true."

"I can't believe my ears!" he shouted. "How can you possibly think you are…are…are that?"

I clenched my teeth and furrowed my brow. *I have to stand firm.* "It's not that I think I'm lesbian, I am lesbian. It's who I am!"

"You need to go to your room and stay there till you change your mind!" Dad said.

"Stephen, Willow, let's calm down. No one needs to go to their room," Mom responded. "Now Honey, I know this can be a confusing time in life. I guess you have friends who are going down this path, too. It's natural to want to be like them."

"Actually, I don't know any lesbians other than Robin, the girl I got into the fight over. So I'm not trying to be like someone else. I'm just trying to be me."

"Well, we can't have you being you. That just won't fly in this family. We are a good Christian family, and it's going to stay that way," Dad said.

"What your father means to say is that we hope you will reconsider this and go back to being the Willow you have always been," Mom added.

"Mom, this is who I have always been. I just haven't been able to admit it to myself until now."

"If we can't talk sense into you, maybe we can punish it into you. You're grounded for a week. Nothing but school and homework. Maybe that will bring you to your senses," Dad said.

"Like grounding's going to change who I am," I responded.

"Go to your room!" he demanded.

Tears were spilling from my eyes by the time I got to my room. I slammed the door.

"I almost lost a nose with that one," Will said, coming in right behind me. "I heard. It wasn't pretty."

"I knew they wouldn't accept me. That's why I haven't told them yet. Now I feel like dirt." I grabbed a tissue, knocking the box to the floor.

"But you're good dirt, the kind that grows good crops."

"Is that supposed to make me feel better?" I couldn't help but laugh. "I guess it's good to know that at least I'm the kind of dirt that's useful."

"You know I love you. The parents will come around, I'm sure. You have to give them time. That was a big shock."

"I didn't get the impression there would be any 'coming around,'" I said, making air quotes. "They're probably going to lock me in a dungeon somewhere before it's all over."

"If they do, I'll bust you out!"

"Thanks! I can always count on you. I don't know what I'd do without you."

He hugged me for the second time today. "I don't know what I'd do without you either. We're a team."

"At least I don't have to go back to in-school suspension tomorrow. Out of one jail and into another."

"I've got to finish up my English paper. Keep the faith!"

I closed the door behind Will and sat on the bed. Taz was in my lap almost instantly. I tried to do homework but couldn't concentrate. Giving up, I pulled out my diary.

Today the inevitable happened. Jaynie turned on me and told Roger. He called my parents and told them. They had a duck fit. Grounded me for a week. Their rejection hurts. My heart knew it was coming, but it still hurts.

At this point I feel like I don't have much left. Will and Myra are the only ones I can count on. The rest of the world seems against me.

My parents' rejection hurts worse than Jaynie's turning on me. She has always seemed a bit shallow. I knew they'd be upset, but I wasn't expecting outright rejection. They wouldn't even talk about it. Dad just went ballistic and sent me to my room. I told Will I feel like dirt.

I couldn't see the page anymore for the tears. The crying intensified to sobs. I buried my face in the pillow to muffle the sound.

Chapter 13

Before school Monday morning, I ran into Myra in the parking lot. "You just had to be out of town on the worst day of my life!"

"You knew we went to my grandparents for Thanksgiving. What are you talking about?"

"Jaynie told Roger that I'm lesbian, so he took Jaynie and me to his office to talk some sense into me." Tears started to fill my eyes. "Then Roger told my parents, and they jumped all over me when I got home. They even grounded me for a week!" I wiped away the one tear that had escaped.

"I'm sorry, Willow. That must have hurt a lot."

More tears escaped, and Myra hugged me.

"I can't believe Jaynie turned on me like that," I said pulling back.

"I imagine she thought she was helping. Jaynie doesn't always have the best problem solving skills."

"Good morning," sounded from behind me, and I jumped. Liia walked into view. "Oh, are you crying? What's wrong?"

I found her accent comforting and sensed her concern was genuine. *I think I can be honest with her.* "Well, you might as well know. I'm lesbian, and my parents found out last night. It wasn't pretty."

"I knew there was something I liked about you," Liia said with a grin. "I'm sorry it didn't go so well with your parents. You'll have to be patient with them."

"Thanks. That's what Will said." *Maybe I have three people on my side, now.* I wiped away more tears. Liia handed me a tissue.

"Dry those tears before you force us to join you," Myra said with a laugh. "We're going to get you through this. I would suggest going to Bellini's after school, but I guess that's out since you're grounded."

"Yeah, I have to go straight home to my new prison."

"I'm home," I called nervously as I walked through the front door. The tension ebbed when silence responded. *Mom must be out.* "Meow," broke the silence, and Taz rubbed against my leg.

Taz continued meowing, which I translated as, "Treats, please." I obliged, and she gobbled them down. I scooped her litter, then went to my room, Taz walking ahead and weaving just in front of my feet.

The house was so quiet that the silence felt heavy. *I wonder if this is what solitary confinement is like. I'm sure this is just the calm before the storm.* I started to turn on music but was afraid I wouldn't hear the garage door open. For some reason, I didn't want to be surprised when Mom or Dad walked in. *Might as well start homework.*

I like to do homework in the order my classes come during the day, so calculus first. I'm not sure how long I had been sitting there when I realized I was staring at one spot on the wall, my thoughts squirming like a bed of snakes. *I'm not getting anywhere.*

I gave up for the time being and pulled out my diary.

I can't concentrate. My feelings and thoughts have the zoomies. My old nemesis is back: Uncertainty. Life would be so much more peaceful if I could be what my parents and the church want. I could go back to the way things used to be. But how hard would that be? Can I squelch my feelings? I would have to live alone my whole life. Never marry. Never love. How that would poison my soul! I wonder what it would be like to have a girlfriend. Is that what I call her?

Maybe I should take Shakespeare's advice: "To thine own self be true." (My English teacher would be proud!) Like Paul said, I'm going to have to fight the good fight and keep the faith.

Lord, I hope you don't mind my using the Bible in reference to my situation. I hope you, at least, still love me. You are the one who created me, you know.

My pen stopped in midair. A welcome wave of calm started in the center of my heart and moved out like a ripple on a lake. I smiled and resumed writing.

Suddenly, the world seems right again. Praying helped. I think I can do this. I know I can do this.

"Supper's ready," sounded through my door. The words caused my heart to speed up. "OK, take three deep breaths. You've got this. Just stay calm," I said to myself before leaving the room.

To my recollection, no one had ever balked at the insistence that we eat supper together as a family, sitting around the table with no TV. It had always been a special time. *I wish I could eat in my room tonight, but I guess it's better to go ahead and face whatever's coming.*

All eyes landed on me when I walked into the kitchen. We sat down, and it was Will's turn to say the blessing.

"Thank you, dear God, for the food, our family and friends, and this time to share together. Amen."

"Did anything interesting happen at school today?" Mom asked.

"I got an A on my English composition," Will answered as he got up to serve his plate. "That was really interesting to me."

"Congratulations," Mom said.

I tried to think of an answer as I followed Will to the stove. "I've made a new friend. Her name is Liia, and she has just moved here from Sweden. She's really nice."

"Congratulations to you, too," Mom said.

"Did anything interesting happen at work today?" Will asked as he sat down.

"I think I got a new client," Mom said with a smile. "They're still looking over the proposal, but they seem interested."

"Way to go, Mom," Will said.

Dad hadn't said a word. *He looks tense.* His brooding increased my stress. I took a bite of mashed potatoes, and my mouth was so dry I had to take a drink of tea to get it down. I glanced at Dad a few times. He seemed focused on eating, so I began to relax.

"Any progress on what we discussed last night?" Dad's question startled me. He was still looking down at his plate.

In a flash of anger I was tempted to be snippy and ask, "And to whom are you talking?" but held my tongue. I put my fork down and took a deep breath.

"I assume you mean have I made any progress on being lesbian. I think I have. I feel more confident today that's who I am. It's good to be feeling more comfortable in my own skin."

"That's not what I mean, and you know it!" Dad snapped. "You are supposed to be realizing that this is wrong and that you need to be what you are supposed to be."

"What if this *is* what I'm supposed to be?" I answered. I could almost see Dad's blood boiling under his skin.

While he was stewing, Mom said, "Willow, please promise that you will take this seriously. We don't want you to jump on the homosexual bandwagon just because it's the latest fad."

I swallowed hard. The words that wanted to rush out were ugly. *I need another deep breath.*

"Mom, homosexuality is not a fad. It's part of how I was created. I can't change who I am." *I'm surprised that came out so calmly.*

"I agree with Willow," Will said. "She would have to deny herself and live a lie just to do what you want her to do."

"Well, I suggest you start lying to yourself because I won't have that in this family!" Dad barked.

It was my blood's turn to boil. "You won't have *THAT* in this family! You can't even say the word! I think you have more work to do on this than I do!"

"Go to your room right now! I won't have you talking back to me!"

"Gladly!" I snapped and stomped to my room.

"Honey, don't you want your plate?" Mom called.

I didn't respond. By the time I got to my room tears soaked my cheeks. I slammed the door for effect, grabbed the box of tissues, and crashed onto the bed.

My tears turned to sobs. No thoughts, just raw feelings flooded my soul. Insistent meows at my door drew me out of that dark hole. I let Taz in and flopped back down. Taz nuzzled me on the cheek and lay down, her back touching my side.

"Thanks, Taz. At least somebody cares."

Chapter 14

Sunday, December 2, 2018

Sunday morning slid in with dull gray skies. The threat of severe storms would be a better match for my mood. *Going to church and youth group feels totally obnoxious. I do have a card to play, though.*

I found Mom in the kitchen when I went for breakfast. "I should be grounded from church and youth group, too. My punishment's not over till this evening."

"Church is exactly where you need to be, young lady. Maybe you will learn something," Mom snapped.

"Ugh! But I don't want to go," I protested and turned to go back to my room. I sat on the bed and stared at the wall with the dread of Roger preaching at me worming through my mind.

Will's signature knock preceded his entrance. "Why protest going to church? At least you get to get out of the house. I'm sure Myra will be there."

"Roger will preach at me again. I'm sure everyone knows he is talking about me. I don't want to be his personal crusade."

"Surely he has moved on by now. Besides, we're going to start talking about Youth Sunday. You want to make sure Myra is nominated to speak."

Will's phone pinged a text. "Hey, Will. It's Myra. Tell Willow I'm looking forward to seeing her today. She'd better show! Tell her I have a surprise for her." A smiley emoji followed.

"Spooky! I think Myra knew we were talking about her. She says you had better come to Sunday school, and she has a surprise for you."

"You're lying. That wasn't her."

Will showed me the text.

"OK, so you weren't lying. It looks like everyone is against me."

"I'd say it's fifty-fifty. Two against and two very much for."

"Thanks, Will. But at church the odds will increase to a hundred and fifty to two."

"I'm sorry this is so hard." He sat on the bed and put his arm around me.

"I don't think I could make it without you and Myra. I wonder what she meant by a surprise."

As Will pulled into the parking place at church, Myra came running up with Liia right behind. I opened the door, and Myra grabbed me in a hug before I was fully out. "Surprise!"

"Hey, Liia! I'm happy to see you."

"I invited Liia to join us," Myra said, stepping back and grinning.

Liia hugged me, too. "Hey. I'm glad to see you."

"I'm feeling so left out," Will pined.

Myra hurried around the car and hugged him. "Better?"

"Yeah. I think I'll make it now."

"Liia, this is my brother, Will."

"It's nice to meet you," she said.

"What an accent!" he said. "It's lovely, by the way."

Liia blushed. "My accent. I wonder if it will ever go away. It makes me so self-conscious."

"I hope it doesn't go away," I said. "I love it!"

"Thanks."

Myra looked at her watch. "We have to hurry!"

We settled into our seats just as Roger began playing the opening chorus on his guitar. *Lord, give me strength.* After the song he led us in a prayer.

"Father God, we are grateful to be here to worship you. Please guide us as we plan for the future. Help all of us to live lives worthy of being called your children. Amen."

That last bit was for me, I bet.

"OK, as you know Youth Sunday is coming up on January twentieth. I know that seems like a long way off, but it will be here before we know it. Our tradition is to nominate someone to give the message. Then we'll fill out the other parts with volunteers. So do we have any nominations?"

"Myra!" Jaynie called out.

"Yay, Myra!" someone else said.

"Myra! Myra! Myra!" the whole group chanted.

Roger waved his arms, signaling for the group to quiet down. "It seems unanimous and enthusiastic that Myra gives the message this year."

Myra raised her hand.

"Please don't tell me that you don't want to do it," Roger pleaded.

"No, I'm honored to speak. I would also like to nominate Willow. We could each do half of it."

Silence hit the room like a tsunami. I actually stopped breathing. I was afraid to look at Myra. I kept my eyes on Roger. His eyes met mine, then he quickly looked away. *He's struggling for a response! I love it!* I glanced at Myra, and she winked. I couldn't help but smile. Roger was now staring out the window.

"The tradition is to have one speaker," Roger said. "I think it would dilute the message to have two different speakers, but I appreciate your nomination. I think we had better stick with Myra. We can let Willow do something else in the service."

I sensed the whole room relax. Roger continued. "I have a list of other duties. Please come up after the lesson and sign up for what you are interested in doing. If the position you want is already filled, please pick another one. If they are all filled, please know that we will all be involved in the music."

After Roger finished the lesson, which was on the season of Advent, I walked with Myra and Liia.

"Thanks for nominating me," I said. "It was fun to watch Roger struggle, even if it was for just a minute."

"Why does Roger not want you to be a part of the service?" Liia asked.

"I think having a gay person in the pulpit is against his religion," I answered.

"I thought we had moved onto the twenty-first century!" Liia huffed. She touched my shoulder. "I'm sorry. I know that being turned down is hard."

I sensed a deep concern in the touch of my new friend. "Thanks, but we all want Myra to be the speaker, anyway."

"I think you would have a lot to add," Myra said. "I just wish Roger could see that."

"We'd better get to church. Tomorrow my grounding is over. Maybe we could celebrate with Bellini's."

I drove Will home after youth group. "At least Roger didn't direct the lesson at me tonight."

"And, your imprisonment ends tonight. You're having a big day!"

"I can't wait to have my phone back. I miss it."

"How have you survived without it for a whole week?"

"You can do a lot on the computer, you know. No texting, but I kept up with social media."

"All under the guise of doing homework, I suppose."

"Of course!"

I parked the car in the driveway. Will hopped out, but I just sat there. He walked around and opened my door. "Aren't you getting out?"

"I'm worried about the next ordeal."

"Two down and one to go!"

"Do you think they'll ground me forever if I don't announce that I'm straight tonight?"

"I don't have a good read on that. They haven't been talking about it. I'm not sure if that is to give you space to decide or if they don't want to hear the answer."

I took three deep breaths before answering the call to supper. "I'm going to stay calm no matter what."

"Yay! Taco salad!" Will said as he sat down at the table. We prayed and built our salads.

There's tension in the air. I can feel it. The conversation around the table started as it usually did on Sundays.

"How was youth group?" Mom asked.

"We started planning for Youth Sunday," Will offered. "Myra is going to speak."

"That's great. She'll do a good job," Mom replied.

I listened to the sound of forks on bowls and wondered when the lecture would start.

"I need some more sour cream please," Will said.

Finally I had to say something. "I guess my grounding is technically up after supper. Do I get my phone back tonight?"

"That depends," Dad said. "Have you made any progress?"

"What do you mean by progress?" I asked, knowing the answer.

"Have you decided to give up this notion and be normal?" he replied.

"It's not a notion. It's who I am, Dad. It's not like deciding to change my major in college."

"Stephen, hon, we talked about this, remember," Mom said. Dad's jaw clenched, and I could see he was fighting back words.

"Willow, this is a big change in your life. Your father and I believe it would be good for you to go for some counseling to help you through this."

"I don't want to go to counseling. I just want to get on with living my new life!"

"It's not an option," Dad said. "If you want to get off being grounded, you will have to get some counseling. We asked Roger, and he has agreed to talk with you."

"I'm not going to Roger for counseling. He has already taken it as his mission to 'fix' me. Anybody but him!"

"I'm sorry you feel that way," Mom said.

A light came on. "How about Ms. Simpson?" I asked.

"Who is that?" Dad asked.

"The school counselor," Mom said. "We could check with her and see if she would have the time to see you."

"We don't know anything about her," Dad argued. "She could be a nutcase."

"She's fine," Will said. "I think she'd be a good choice."

"I think she is someone I could open up to. I had to see her during my in-school suspension," I added, hoping to keep the momentum going. I noticed I was holding my fork in midair as I leaned into the silence. I put it on the table so I wouldn't look so silly.

"I think that would be a good compromise," Mom offered.

My palms began to sweat while I waited for Dad to reply.

"I would rather you talk to Roger to make sure you get a Christian perspective, but we'll give this a try," he said.

"OK, then. I'll talk to her in the morning and see what we can set up," I said with relief.

"One of us will talk to her, too. I want to be sure this is actually happening," Dad barked.

"Thanks for the trust," I hissed and left the table. I didn't let the grin show till I got back to my room. *I think I'll like talking to Ms. Simpson! She may actually be able to help me through this transition.*

Chapter 15

In the predawn darkness of Monday morning, I awoke in a sweat. I was breathing hard. The clock said 4:37. I threw off the covers to cool down, disturbing Taz.

It was a dream. Thank God! I rolled over and tried to go back to sleep. I tossed and turned, but sleep wouldn't come. I peeked at the clock again. 4:53.

I give up. It looks like it's diary time again. I pulled out the diary.

I had a horrible dream. They wanted me to be a swimmer, but I wanted to fly on the hang gliders. They kept catching me and throwing me into the water. At first it was a pool. Then it was a lake. The water was so cold. The last time they threw me in, I thought I was going to drown. I couldn't get back to the surface. I was so tired. I think that's when I woke up.

Thinking about the dream made me anxious. Feelings crystallized into thoughts, and I resumed writing.

I think the dream means I'm resisting doing what people want me to do. I wonder what that could be about! The question is, am I better off just getting in the water and being what people want? Or is it better to keep fighting to be who I really am? How can I 'honor thy parents' if I don't accede to their expectations? Parents are supposed to 'train up a child in the way they should go.' So should I listen to them and be what they expect. But they are also supposed to love their children. Can't they love me for who I really am and not just if I'm what they want me to be? Why does this have to be so hard?!!!!!

I plopped back onto the pillow from my cross-legged position. My mind raced, thoughts and feelings swirling together like a building tornado. I had more to write.

It's 5:07 in the morning. I'm sitting in my bed writing about a bad dream. Maybe there is wisdom in my parents wanting me to get counseling. I hope it will help me decide whether to swim or fly.

I locked the diary and put it away. *That was intense!* Lying back down, I was able to relax. The screech of the alarm was the next thing to register.

"Where were you at break?" Myra asked as she and Liia caught up with me after school.

"My parents insist that I get counseling for my 'condition,' so I had to see Ms. Simpson about setting up some appointments. I think they're hoping counseling will 'fix' me."

"Did you tell them that there is nothing to fix? I think you are fine the way you are," Liia said.

I was touched by Liia's comment. "Thanks!"

"At least Ms. Simpson's nice," Myra added.

"They wanted me to get counseling from Roger, but I nipped that idea in the bud!"

"Wow! I can't imagine how much fun that would be!" Myra responded with a laugh. "At least you aren't grounded anymore. Are we still on for Bellini's?"

"I wouldn't miss it!"

"Hey, Jaynie!" Myra called out. "We're going to Bellini's. Want to come?"

I noticed a hesitation in Jaynie's response.

"Are all three of you going?" she asked.

"Yeah! Come on and make it a foursome! We'll fill a whole table!" Myra encouraged.

"I'm sorry to miss out, but I have to do some research for next year's color guard formations. Maybe next time." She turned and headed toward the gym.

"That was interesting," I said.

"What do you mean?" Myra asked."

"I think she didn't want to go because of me. You saw how she hesitated."

"I think we can add paranoia to your list of personality traits! That's just Jaynie."

"How often has she turned us down before? Research for color guard formations! That's ridiculous!"

"That does seem like a weak excuse," Liia said. "What is color guard, anyway?"

"They dance and twirl flags to the band's music during halftime at football games," Myra explained.

"American football," I clarified.

"You have football in high school?"

"Of course. We have soccer, too," I said.

"I still have lots to learn," Liia laughed.

When we walked into Bellini's, Lacey said from behind the counter, "Dark chocolate cherry and mint chocolate chip for Willow and Myra coming up. I'm afraid I haven't learned your favorite or your name."

"I'm Liia, and I'd like dulce de leche, please."

"I'm on it!"

"You don't really think Jaynie didn't come because of you, do you?" Myra asked after her first bite.

"That's what it looked like to me."

"I think we need more data before we can make that decision," Myra said.

"She means we will have to see what happens a few more times when we invite Jaynie to do something that involves me," I translated for Liia.

"I'm not as dumb as I look," she answered. "I knew that's what she meant. And I think she is right. You can't make sweeping conclusions about a person based on one instance."

"OK, maybe I am paranoid," I said. "I'll give her another chance. But my gut tells me I'm right."

We finished the gelatos, and Liia asked, "Can I get a ride home, Willow? If not, I can call my dad."

"Sure! I'll be glad to."

I parked my Jeep in Liia's driveway.

"Would you mind coming in to meet my dad? I'd love for him to meet you."

I checked my watch. "I'm supposed to meet Will for tennis, but I think I have time for that. It won't kill him if he has to wait a few minutes."

"Dad's an author, so he's always home unless he has to go to Sweden to meet with his publisher or do a book tour," Liia said as she led me to the door.

"Why did you move to America, if your dad's books are based out of Sweden?"

"Mom's work transferred her here to help develop a new line of batteries for power tools." Liia opened the door. "After you."

She called out in Swedish. Looking at me, she explained, "Sorry. We speak Swedish at home a lot. I just let Dad know you are here."

I heard footsteps, then a thin, blond haired man appeared in the kitchen.

"God dag!" He said. "I'm Lars. It is a pleasure to meet you, and I'm guessing you are Willow."

"I am, and it's a pleasure to meet you, too. I'm enjoying getting to know Liia."

"I am glad to hear that. We worried about her making friends in a new country."

"As you can see, I have a nice one in Willow," Liia said and put her arm around my shoulder.

I returned the gesture. "I'm glad she came our way."

"I see," he said with a grin. "If you will excuse me, I must get back to the computer. My publisher is serious about her deadlines." With that he disappeared, and I soon heard the faint clicks of the keyboard.

"Wow! He types really fast."

"He certainly has had plenty of practice."

I discovered I still had my arm around Liia and let go.

"You have to let me show you my room! It won't be an official visit if you don't." She grabbed my hand and pulled me down the hallway.

The door opened to a cheery room with sky blue walls, teal paisley bedspread, and posters everywhere.

"Wow! I'm guessing these are pictures of Sweden."

"I thought it would help me feel more at home, so I covered my room with them. These are places in Upsala, where we used to live. I loved going down by the river," she said and pointed to a poster of the Fyris River. "This one is my favorite."

"It's beautiful." I checked my watch. "I was supposed to meet Will ten minutes ago! I'd better text him. I enjoyed getting to meet your dad and see your room."

"I wish you could stay a little longer."

We stepped outside, and the sound of raindrops greeted my ears. "Now that changes things." Pulling out my phone, I texted Will. "Sorry I'm late, but I guess that's a moot point since it's raining. See you at the house."

"Would you like to stay and do some calculus?"

"Calculus is always better with company! Let me text Mom." We stood on the front porch watching the rain and waited for Mom's reply.

"I love to watch it rain," she said. "It makes me feel peaceful."

My phone pinged. "Good grief! She wants to know who you are."

I texted back, "She's my new friend from Sweden. I've told you about her."

"OK, but be careful," was the reply.

"Yay, I can stay! But she told me to be careful. I never considered doing calculus dangerous. I guess I could poke myself with the pencil." We laughed.

Liia added, "Or maybe get a paper cut."

We set up on the kitchen table, books open and paper out. I looked over the first problem. "This is almost as bad as my dream last night."

"You had a bad dream?"

I told her about it and how I felt when I woke up.

"That's horrible!"

"At least the day is ending better than it started."

Chapter 16

Sunday, December 9, 2018

I'm going to ace him! I drew back and put all of my power into the serve. The ball hit the left corner of the service box like lightning.

"Dang, girl!" Will said after crashing into the fence trying to return it. "That was wicked!"

"I was feeling at one with the court!"

"I hope you have that feeling at state!"

"I hope we make it to state. That's the first step, you know."

"Oh, ye of little faith! We'll make it!"

"Speaking of making it, we'd better go if we're going to get to youth group."

"I'm sorry Roger wouldn't let you speak on Youth Sunday. What did you end up signing up for?"

"I signed up for the prayer. I figured no one else would want to do that anyway."

"I signed up to be a greeter. No pressure!"

"Who knows what today is?" Roger was asking as we walked in.

"I told you we'd be late," I whispered.

"Glad you two could make it," Roger said, then repeated his question.

"It's Sunday," John answered, and everyone laughed.

"Funny, John," Roger said. "It's the second Sunday in Advent. If you were paying attention, you noticed we lit the second candle on the wreath during worship. Today is the day we focus on John the Baptist's call to repentance.

"This is a time of repentance when we get our hearts ready to receive the Messiah who is about to be born. Each of us has to look into our hearts, find the things we need to repent of, and start rooting them out of our lives. If we can do that, we will be ready for the birth of our Savior."

Roger led a prayer then said, "I appreciate everyone who signed up for the duties for Youth Sunday. There are a couple of opportunities still open. So if you didn't get a chance last week, please come up and check out the list after we're through."

He led the closing song and prayer, then asked, "Willow, could I see you a minute?"

My heart turned to lead. *Now what?*

"I'm coming with you," Myra whispered.

"Me, too," Liia added.

"If you don't mind, I need to speak to Willow alone," Roger said as we walked up.

"I see you signed up for the prayer," Roger said after Myra and Liia retreated.

"Yes. I doubted anyone else would want to do that."

"I hate to say this, but given what you are, I don't think that would be appropriate. I don't think the church folks would approve, and I don't want to create…" He paused and appeared to be searching for the right word. "Controversy."

"Given what I am? What's that supposed to mean?" My dread turned to anger. "I am the same person I have always been, and I believe God loves me. I can't imagine God would mind me praying!"

"Calm down. Why don't you be a greeter? I think it would be cute to have the twins as greeters."

"I think you have some repenting to do!" I turned and stormed out of the room. I heard footsteps hurrying behind me. *I hope he's not coming after me!*

"What was that about?" Myra asked. I breathed a sigh of relief when it wasn't Roger.

"He won't even let me do the prayer. He's afraid it will create 'controversy.' This is just so hard. I should just say I'm straight so everything can go back to the way it was." The blasted tears were back.

"We'll just see about that! I'm going to have a talk with Roger," Myra said and headed back to the youth room.

I could hear her from the hallway. "I think you need to reconsider banishing Willow from saying the prayer at Youth Sunday. She has just as much right as anyone to be up there. I think it was tacky enough that you wouldn't let us do the message together. But this is ridiculous!"

"I understand. It's a hard decision for me. Let me think about it some more."

"I hope you're serious and will really reconsider," Myra said.

"You go girl!" Will shouted as Myra came back to the group.

"He said he'd reconsider. I hope he wasn't just blowing me off."

Hope surged in my heart.

"Chin up, Willow," Will said. "Life is worth fighting for. Besides, you know we love you." He punched me in the arm.

"Yeah, but you're stuck with me!" I punched him back.

Dad was coming in from the deck as we walked into the house. "The fire is just right! It's time to put these babies on," he said, grabbing the steaks off the counter.

"Don't get in too big a hurry. The potatoes have twenty more minutes," Mom advised.

"Perfect! You can't rush a filet mignon."

"Looks like dinner is in twenty minutes, then," Mom confirmed.

We sat down to eat. After Mom said the blessing, Dad asked, "Did anything exciting happen at youth group?"

"I wouldn't say exciting, but it was eventful," Will said.

I cringed and shot Will a look to tell him I didn't want to talk about it.

"We just about have Youth Sunday planned out," he explained.

I knew he understood my look and appreciated the deflection. But it wasn't enough. Mom zeroed in on the "eventful" part.

"That doesn't sound eventful. What else happened?"

"If you must know, Roger refused to let me say the prayer during the service," I answered, trying to keep my voice calm. "Myra and I wanted to do the message together, but he wouldn't allow that either."

"I see," Dad said. "You will have to understand that there are consequences to your behavior. If you are going to persist with this homosexuality stuff, then a lot of doors will close to you. That's just the way it is."

"Just because 'that's the way it is' doesn't make it right. Why shouldn't I be able to give the message or say the prayer? Is it because all of you consider me a sinner? I think Paul said we are all sinners. So am I a worse sinner than the rest of you?" My voice was rising, but I couldn't help it. It was too late.

"Don't raise your voice to me, young lady," Dad said. "Homosexuality is just not acceptable in the church. It takes sin too far. And as far as I can tell, homosexual people aren't trying to fix their sin. They just wallow in it and enjoy taunting God."

"What if it's not a sin at all? What if God made me this way because this is how God wants me to be? It's not like I woke up one morning and decided, 'Hum, I think I'll change and be gay now.' It's been a part of me all along. I know now that I tried to bury it so I could fit in and meet your expectations."

"I don't think the counseling is helping. Maybe we need to try someone else," Mom said.

"I've only had one session with her!" I nearly shouted. "And I think it will help, but not like you want it to. I think she can help me make my way through all the rejection I am getting from those who are supposed to love me."

My fists were clenched under the table, fingernails digging into my palms. *Relax.* I wanted to get up and run to my room but knew that wouldn't help. *I can't run. I'm going to have to fight for my place in the world.*

"Honey, you know we love you," Mom said. "We just want what's best for you."

"Then quit trying to mold me into something I'm not. Just let me be me." My fists clenched again.

"That's exactly what we are trying to do," Dad said. "We want you to go back to being you and get this ridiculous idea out of your head."

"Ugh! It's not an idea! How many times do I have to say that? I didn't want to be gay! I didn't decide to be gay! I just am gay! You talk like my being gay is like deciding all of a sudden to wear a different style of clothes. Well it's not. It's who I am, how I was created. It's not something I can change or be talked out of. We are all just going to have to live with it."

"Well pardon me if I'm not ready to see my daughter ruin her life," Dad snipped.

"I know y'all think this is terrible, but she is not ruining her life," Will offered. "If she tries to deny herself and live like she is straight, then she will ruin it."

"Honey, this is a big decision that will affect the rest of your life. Your dad and I just want you to consider it carefully."

"It's not a decision, I keep trying to tell you! It's a matter of being… It's who I am!"

"I think you need to go to your room and cool off," Dad said.

"Gladly!" I stormed out of the kitchen, nearly knocking over my chair as I got up. I landed on the bed face first. This time the tears came from anger more than hurt. Taz hopped onto my back, kneaded a few times, then lay down.

"I may lose my parents, but at least I'll still have you."

Chapter 17

A cold wind whistled through the trees. I zipped my jacket on my way to meet Myra and Liia outside for break.

"Whose idea was it to meet outside today?" I asked.

"Yeah, it's cold!" Myra added.

"Give me a break. This is nothing," Liia smiled, unfazed by the chilly weather.

"Your blood is still adjusted to Sweden's weather. This is rough on us southern girls," I said and noticed Jaynie coming out the door. Our eyes met, and Jaynie turned around and went back in.

"What's up with her?" I asked.

"With whom?" Myra responded, her back toward the door.

"Jaynie started to come out then turned around," I answered, pushing my hands into my pockets. "I think she has officially turned against me."

"She asked me not to tell you, but since you've already figured it out, I guess I can. Her parents told her they don't want her associating with you since you're gay. And I'm afraid she agrees with them."

"But she's one of my best friends! How could she do that?" The hurt felt like a stone in my heart. Cold fingers spread out through my chest. My legs lost their strength, and I was sinking to the ground. My vision blurred.

As if from far away I heard voices, "Are you OK?"

"Willow, I think you're about to pass out."

Someone had me by the shoulders. A forehead pressed against mine. I could finally make out Liia's face. "Come on, Willow. It will be OK," she was saying.

Myra's face came into view. "Do you think you can stand up?" Her arm went around my back. Things were clearing. *How did I end up on the ground?*

"I think so." Myra and Liia helped me to my feet.

"What happened?" Myra asked.

"I think I fainted."

"Well, I knew that, but why?"

"It just hurts so bad that Jaynie has turned away. Is she never going to talk to me?"

"I think she'll come around. We have to give her some time."

"And a good scolding," Liia added.

"I've already done that. I told her that she needs to learn to love the new you just as much as the old you. That is her Christian responsibility. So far it hasn't seemed to help," Myra said.

"Are you steady enough for us to let go?" Liia asked.

"Yeah. I'm still sad, though."

The bell rang, and we headed to class. I stopped by English composition and showed Ms. Price the note from Ms. Simpson about releasing me for a counseling session.

"OK. I'll see you when you get back."

I knocked on the open door, and Ms. Simpson looked up. A warm smile brightened her face. "Good morning!" she said as she pushed back her black hair and removed her glasses. "Come in and close the door, please."

I sat down with a heavy heart but managed, "Good morning."

"You seem down today."

I looked into Ms. Simpson's bright blue eyes and sensed compassion. "I just learned that one of my best friends will no longer associate with me because I'm gay."

"I'm sorry to hear that, but you need to know that is common. You can expect to lose some friends and gain others. Tell me how that made you feel."

I tried to speak, but tears rushed ahead of the words.

"Take your time. It is OK to grieve over the loss of a friend."

My tears turned to sobs. It felt like they would never stop. Finally they slowed, subsided, and I could talk. "It has been so hard the last few weeks. I'm so tired of crying!"

Once I started, the words poured like the tears. "My parents are against me. Our youth minister wouldn't let me speak on Youth Sunday, and now he won't let me say the prayer either. Today Jaynie turned on me. I feel like all I get is rejection."

"That is a hard place to be. I can imagine it hurts a lot."

"It does hurt a lot. My parents expect you to talk me into being straight again. They want me back the way I was. Sometimes I wonder if that would be the easier path."

"For whom would it be easier?" Ms. Simpson asked, leaning back in her chair.

"That's an interesting question." I stopped and pondered. "I know it would be easier for everyone else, but would it be easier for me?"

"You have played the role of being straight for a long time. It's familiar."

"Now that I know I'm gay, I don't think it would be as easy. I had it hidden so deep down inside that I didn't even know I was playing a role. I think I would loathe myself if I tried to go back."

"When you're a caring soul, which I believe you are, it's hard to let other people struggle because of you. What you need to realize is that is their battle, not yours."

"They sure make it feel like my battle."

"You presented them with a change, a challenge, and they are trying to figure out what to do with it. The easiest course is to restore the status quo. That costs them nothing, so that's what people tend to try first."

"Do you think they will come around?" I asked, dreading the answer.

"I can't answer for other people. Typically, some will and some won't."

"So I just have to carry on and let the chips fall where they may?"

"No, you have to keep engaging and building bridges to the ones who are important, let them know you want to be in their lives. Then be prepared to live with their decisions."

"So you think I should reach out to Jaynie?"

"Sure, if she is important in your life."

"But she turned and walked the other way when she saw me. She won't even talk to me now."

"You could always text her. She will have to see that."

A slow smile spread on my face. "That's a great idea! Now all I have to do is figure out what to say."

"I would recommend not being judgmental. Just tell her how you feel."

"Thanks! I'll try that."

"I look forward to seeing you next week," Ms. Simpson said, standing and extending her hand.

I shook her hand and said, "You helped me a lot today."

"I'm glad to hear that. It's what I'm here for."

I went back to English composition. I tried to focus on Ms. Price but kept rehearsing what I could say to Jaynie. Before I knew it, class was over.

"Supper time!" sounded from the kitchen. I moved my chair back from the desk, and Taz hopped down from my lap.

"I believe it is Willow's turn to say the blessing," Dad said.

"Dear God, thank you for friends, family, and this food you have provided. And thank you for Ms. Simpson. Amen."

"So you talked to Ms. Simpson today?" Mom asked. "How did that go?"

"It was great. She's very insightful."

"How was she helpful?" Mom asked.

I paused, conflicted about what to say. *I think I'll tell them about Jaynie.* "Jaynie's parents told her she has to stop talking with me. When she saw me at break today, she turned and walked the other way. That really hurt." *I'll skip the part about passing out!*

"Ms. Simpson recommended that I reach out to Jaynie by text and let her know that I still want to be her friend and don't want to lose her. Then she said that I have to realize that the decision is Jaynie's and not mine. I'll have to live with what she decides."

I stopped there, forcing my tongue to be still rather than adding, "If people choose to reject me because of my homosexuality, the problem is theirs." *I suspect that would get me sent to my room!*

"See what happens when you do such a rash thing?" Dad said. "You will probably lose a lot of friends the longer you keep at this. You could save yourself a lot of heartache if you would just go back to being the old Willow we used to know."

Tension built, threatening to close my throat. My voice sounded hoarse and weak when I said, "I just can't see that happening, Dad. Gay is who I am. It's who I've always been. I just kept it stuffed down so deep inside that I didn't realize it." I braced for the response but speaking those words gave me a sense of power. I straightened my spine and readied myself.

"Willow, you know that is against our faith. I just don't understand how you could do this. It's just not right."

Rather than anger, I sensed pain in dad's voice. "I'm sorry, Dad, but it's not really something I am doing. It's not like deciding to do drugs. This is about who I am, how I was created."

"Don't try to pin this on God!" The anger flashed. "I'll have no talk of that, and I don't want my daughter living in sin. I'll have no talk of that either!"

"But…" I started.

"End of discussion!" Dad barked.

A heavy silence fell over the table that I didn't dare break.

Chapter 18

Sunday, December 16, 2018

Scratching Taz on the ear, I said, "Be a good kitty, and we'll be back after church."

"Meow."

"No, you've already had your morning treats."

I was whistling "I Stand Amazed in the Presence," while I put on my coat. The door popped open, and Will's head poked in.

"You're in a good mood today."

"I guess I am."

"Any idea why?"

"I'm trusting that Roger has reconsidered and will let me do the prayer for Youth Sunday. That'll be a small victory."

"I hope you're right."

"Come on. Let's go," Dad called from the kitchen.

Myra and Jaynie were talking in the parking lot when we pulled up. I tensed. *Will she walk away again? That would look really bad at church!*

I tried to read Jaynie's face as I walked up and said, "Hey."

"Hey," they replied together.

"I meant what I said in the text. I want us to stay friends. You are so important to me."

"I want to stay friends, too," she said. "It just seems so wrong. We've been taught all our lives that is against God's will."

"Maybe we were taught wrong," I replied. "It's not something I can do anything about. It's not like trying to stop doing drugs or being racist."

"My parents don't want me to even talk with you."

"Willow is the same Willow she was a few months ago. She has just learned more about herself," Myra added.

I watched Jaynie's face contort. I could see the conflict in her soul, and that gave me hope. *Patience!* The silence was awkward.

"Let me think about it. I'd better go before my parents see me." With that, she hustled into the church.

"Well that was awkward," Myra said.

"But at least she will think about it," I felt my muscles relax. "What do your parents say about me?"

"They haven't said anything. I haven't mentioned the change, so I don't know if they've heard," Myra replied and put her hands in her pockets. "We'd better go in before we're late."

Roger was leading the class in "O Come All Ye Faithful" when we walked in.

"It's just the first verse," Myra whispered. We sat down and joined in the singing.

I wish I felt joyful and triumphant. The fact is I'm nervous and my palms are clammy. My heart is pounding. I need to calm down! I'll just have to live with whatever Roger decides. It will be OK. Breathe!

"Youth Sunday is only five weeks away. I know that seems like a long time, but once Christmas is past we will have just four to go. Myra, have you thought about your message?"

"I have a couple of ideas rolling around. I'll have more time to work on it over Christmas break. And yes, I'll work on it. I plan to have it ready before we start back to school in January."

"Great! I'm happy to help if you need me to. We just about have all of the positions filled. We do still need a couple of greeters. If there aren't any volunteers, I'll draft you!

"OK, today is the third Sunday in Advent, so the lesson is on John the Baptist's message. Jaynie, please read Luke 3:7-18."

Jaynie looked around. Someone passed her a Bible. "Give me a minute," she said as she searched for the passage. She read through the text.

"John says that repentance is not enough. It's not enough to realize that we are sinners and ask for forgiveness. We are also expected to go on and live a life worthy of the repentance. What do you think that means?"

"He is saying that we need to care for the people around us, especially those who are hurting," Will answered.

"Exactly! Just as Jesus would go on to say, 'Love your neighbor as yourself,' John is already telling us to do that. Loving God and loving our neighbors becomes the cornerstone of the Gospel," Roger said.

"Does that mean we are supposed to love everybody? 'Cause I know some people who aren't very loveable," Wyatt quipped.

"Do you know anyone whom God has created that God doesn't love?" Roger asked. " If God loves everyone, then that's what we are called to do."

I wish he would practice what he preaches!

Just before Roger dismissed the class he said, "Remember the sign-up sheet is on the board. We need at least two more greeters."

I was sweating when I went to check the sign-up sheet. My heart froze when I saw the name by prayer: Jaynie.

"Oh no," Myra said looking over my shoulder.

My jaw clenched, and my fists tightened.

"I'm sorry," I heard Myra say as I turned toward Roger.

"I see you don't consider me worthy to even say the prayer on Youth Sunday. That's a fine example of loving your neighbor!" My voice rose with each word.

"Just calm down. That's not how it is. I just can't let someone… like you be in the chancel and speaking. I love you, but there are limits to what we can let you do in church."

My heart thudded in my chest. My nails dug into my palms. I wanted to scream. I wanted to lash out at Roger and tell him how wrong he was, but no words came. I turned and stormed out of the room.

"How could you do that to me?" I hissed as I passed Jaynie.

"I'm sorry. Roger asked me to do the prayer. I didn't know you wanted to." Jaynie's words faded as I stomped away.

I was pounding the poor picnic table again when I heard Will say, "You might need these." "These" being my purse and coat. I hadn't even noticed I was cold.

"Thanks." I pulled the coat on and wiped more tears.

Myra wrapped her arms around me. "You're a good person. Don't let Roger's negativity get you down. You have to rise above that."

I hugged her back. Tears flowed, but I still had no words to say.

Will wrapped his arms around both of us. "You're still number one in my book."

I began to calm and control returned to my soul. "I don't know what I would do without you two. You're my anchors."

"That's right, and we're not going to let you get blown away," Myra offered.

Sounds of the organ and first hymn floated through the air.

"It's cold out here. We should move this party inside," Will said as he zipped his coat.

"I'm not going to church. I just can't."

"At least come inside where it's warm. You could sit in a classroom," Will coaxed.

"No. Tell Mom and Dad I walked home."

"Girl, you can't walk home in those pumps," Myra observed.

"Watch me."

"Don't be crazy. You don't have to go to the service, but stay inside and ride home with us," Will pleaded.

"I'm going home." I set off walking out of the parking lot. *I've had enough church today.*

I heard Will say to Myra, "Tell our parents what happened. The next thing I knew, he was walking beside me.

"What are you doing?"

"You don't think I could let my number one sister do something this rash by herself, do you?"

I bumped him with my shoulder, my heart warming. "Thanks." We set off on the long walk together.

Chapter 19

Sunday, December 16, 2018

*M*y little toes are both hurting. We've gone less than a mile. This can't be good. I kept walking, refusing to give in to the pain. I could feel the blisters growing as we walked. After another quarter of a mile, I couldn't ignore the pain anymore. I pulled off my left shoe and looked. The little toe was bloody.

"Ouch!" Will said. "We have a long way to go. Do you think you can make it?"

"I don't have a choice. At least these are just kitten heels." I winced as I slid the shoe back on. "Let's press on."

"You're limping."

"Tell me about it." I noticed Will scanning the area.

"Look, there's the Waffle House!"

"I'm not hungry."

"Maybe not, but they have seats."

"Sitting down won't get me home."

"Sure it will. You sit down, have a coffee or coke, and I'll walk home and get my car. Before you know it you'll be home bandaging those toes."

I pulled off my right shoe. Another bloody toe. "Give me your shoulder while I put this shoe back on."

I felt defeated. What had started out as a protest ended up with Will's having to rescue me. *I can't see any other sensible way out of this.* "OK. I give. I'm sorry. I should have listened to Myra, but I just couldn't face church knowing that I'm not wanted there."

"I just wish everyone could see the wonderful you that I know. Then there wouldn't be any problems."

"Thanks. You're the best brother ever."

"OK, hop on."

"I'm not going into Waffle House on your back."

"OK, I'll let you off at the door."

"You're crazy."

"I'm waiting."

I hesitated. *This is ridiculous.* Then I hopped onto his back. "Getty-up!"

I was sitting on the side of the tub drying my poor toes. Will was standing by with antibiotic ointment when sound boomed from the kitchen.

"Will! Willow!" It was Dad.

"Uh-oh," Will whispered. "Time for the inquisition."

I had to stifle a laugh. "We're back here."

Mom appeared first, her face a mixture of fear and anger. "What happened to your toes?"

Dad was right behind. I saw only anger in his eyes. "What's going on?" he demanded.

Will started the explanation. "Willow was upset because Roger won't let her say the prayer for Youth Sunday. She couldn't stop crying and didn't want to go to church in that state, so we tried to walk home. She got blisters, so I put her in Waffle House and came home for the car."

"Move," Mom said, pushing by Will to get to me. "Let me see those." She knelt down and inspected my feet. "Let me help you."

"I can put a Band-Aid on, Mom. But thanks."

She stood back up.

"If you two ever pull a stunt like that again, there will be serious consequences," Dad grumped.

"I asked Myra to tell you what we were doing," I responded.

"She did, but I still don't approve of this. Who knows what could have happened."

"Hawksville is not exactly a dangerous town," Will said.

"Don't argue with me!" Dad barked and walked down the hall.

"I don't think I'll be playing tennis today," I said to Will.

"After that stunt, you two won't be going anywhere but to youth group," Mom said.

I slipped and got the Band-Aid stuck on itself. "Hand me another one." Nausea rolled in. *I'm not sure if it's the thought of going to youth group or the toes.* I started to tell Mom that I couldn't go back but resisted. *I need a plan.* I finally succeeded with getting the last toe bandaged.

Mom left, and Will put away the bandages and ointment.

"I don't think I can stand going to youth group," I whispered. "I have to come up with a plan."

"Oh no! Not another plan! Let's just go. Myra will be there," he encouraged.

"Why would I want to go listen to Roger as he slips in little judgmental barbs?"

"Because if you don't, he wins."

"What do you mean, 'he wins?'"

"He will have successfully run you off."

"Hmm. I hadn't thought of it that way."

The sound of a frog croaking let me know I had a call. "Hey, Myra," I said, walking to my room.

"Are you OK? Did you make it home?"

"My pride is injured worse than my toes, but other than that I'm fine."

"Why is your pride injured?"

"I couldn't make it home. I had to sit at the Waffle House while Will got the car."

"I told you not to walk in those shoes!"

"I know. I should've listened. Why do we have to wear shoes that injure our feet?"

"I'm sure it started with men not wanting us to be able to get away from them. Somewhere along the line women decided that they look good."

"I think it's time to change the fashion and wear something comfortable."

"Maybe you could design a line of dressy looking sneakers!"

"That's a great idea!"

"Now seriously, how are you doing with the Roger rejection?"

"Not good. I don't want to go to youth group tonight. I was thinking I'd work up a plan to skip it without Mom and Dad finding out. Will said if I do, then Roger wins."

"Please come. I need you there."

"I don't want to face Roger knowing that he looks down on me."

"I can certainly understand that, but you know that we support you. Don't throw out the good because of one bad apple."

"OK, but if he directs the lesson at me, I may lose it."

"Great! I'll see you this afternoon."

"I'm on lunch duty," Will called, walking down the hall. "Grilled ham, tomato, and cheese sandwiches. If that's not OK, speak now or forever hold your peace!"

I smiled. *I wish I could be as good a person as Will.* A wave of guilt flooded my heart. I plopped onto the bed, feeling heavy. *Why do I feel guilty?* thumped in my brain. My heart continued to sink. *I feel like I'm letting everyone down. My parents, Jaynie, even Roger. Not that long ago, I was someone they all liked. Now I'm the great disappointment.*

Taz's rubbing along my back pulled me from my dark thoughts. She looped around and rubbed my chin.

"Thanks," I said, rubbing Taz along her back. "I think life is simpler for a cat. You just love no matter what. Or maybe you are wiser than humans."

"Come and get 'em while they're hot!" Will called from the kitchen.

He had the sandwiches on a plate covered with foil and the table set. "Will, you're too good to be true."

"You haven't changed clothes! What were you doing back there all this time?"

"I was sitting on the bed feeling low."

"You should feel low after pulling a stunt like that!" Dad said, walking into the kitchen. "I'm glad Will had the good sense to go with you."

"Thanks for lunch," Mom said. "Why didn't you just wait in a classroom till church was over?"

"Because I was too hurt to stay. I had to get out of there. Now I'm feeling guilty. I'm letting everybody down." Tears threatened, but I fought them back.

"If you'd stop this homosexual nonsense, you'd feel better about yourself," Dad said.

Rage mixed with my guilt. Mom added, "I'm sorry we've been pushing you so hard. Maybe we need to just let you grow out of this."

I couldn't believe my ears! "Grow out of this? Have you not been listening? This isn't something I'm going to 'grow out of!'" I said, making air quotes.

"I just don't understand how you could change so suddenly. One day you're a normal teenager. The next day you say you're homosexual. How can that be?"

"That's not the way it is, Mom! I don't even want to be gay. It's just the way I am. I think I didn't realize it sooner because of all the pressure society puts on people to be straight, to be normal like you said. I had to keep it stuffed down below my consciousness so I could fit in."

I noticed Dad's jaw clenching. He wasn't eating.

"I still don't understand why you think you're homosexual," Mom said.

"You know how you're always going on about how good looking you think Brad Pitt is?"

"Yeah, so?"

"I think Scarlett Johansson is really hot." I wasn't expecting the heavy silence that followed.

Dad picked up his sandwich. "That's enough of that. Let's just eat in peace."

Giddiness bloomed in the center of my chest and started to grow. I swallowed, trying to stop a smile but smiled anyway. I picked up my sandwich and a snort escaped. They all looked. I tried to stifle it, but a full laugh followed.

"What is so funny, young lady?" Dad asked. Will was grinning, too.

"I don't know. Maybe it's that this is the first time I've ever told anyone that I think Scarlett Johansson is hot."

Will burst out laughing, and Dad cut him a stern look. "You have both lost your minds. No more of that kind of talk at the table. We are supposed to be a Christian family."

"This is the day that the Lord has made. Let us rejoice and be glad in it!" *I can't believe I just said that!* Dad's jaw clenched hard. I braced myself for an explosion. There was only silence.

Chapter 20

Sunday, December 16, 2018

I walked slowly across the church parking lot. My toes were tender, but my heart was more so. I didn't even realize I had stopped.

"Do I need to carry you?" Will asked.

"I shouldn't be here." It was my heart and not the toes that had stopped me. "I can't go in."

"You promised Myra you'd come, so come on."

I forced my feet to move. It felt like trying to move two magnets with the same polarity together. The church seemed to be pushing me away.

"Take some deep breaths and just ignore Roger. You'll be OK."

"I hope you're right. If I start to lose it, drag me out of there."

"It's a deal. But if I start dragging, you have to come along and not resist."

"Deal."

By the time we made it to the youth room, they were finishing the opening round of songs. I settled next to Myra, Liia, and Jaynie. Will sat with Sandra.

"Better late than never," Roger said as he put down his guitar. "Tonight I want us to focus on an amazing passage from Isaiah. Someone read Isaiah 9:2-7."

"I've got it," Rachel said. She went on to read, "The people who walked in darkness have seen a great light; those who lived in a land of deep darkness—on them light has shined…"

"Isaiah describes Jesus' coming, his birth into our world, as a light shining in darkness. There is a lot of darkness in the world. People are hurting and struggling in so many ways. What is some of the darkness you see around you?"

"I saw a homeless person on my way to youth group," Myra answered.

"People with cancer," Wyatt said.

"There are a lot of people starving in Africa," Alice offered.

"All of the people trying to get into the US at our southern border. They are trying to get away from dangerous situations," Daniel said.

"These are great examples," Roger resumed.

I forced my fists to relax when no one called out homosexuality as a sign of darkness.

Roger continued, "The hardships we face make our worlds dark. But sin also makes our world dark. If we choose to sin and stay away from God we live in darkness. How many of us are sinners?"

"All of us," Myra said.

"That's right. We all sin and fall short of the glory of God. So when we believe, we have one foot in darkness and one in light. Yet now that Jesus is not physically here, you and I are called to be the light for the world.

"If we are half in the light and half in the dark, how are we supposed to bring light to the world?"

"Love. We have to love others as Jesus loves us," Will answered.

"Perfect!" Roger said. "None of us are pure like Jesus, but we can all try to love as he did. And guess what, when we do that, we move more into the light. So go out there and love on people and let them see the light of Jesus in you. Who knows how many lives you can change."

Roger dismissed us, and Myra whispered, "See, that wasn't so bad."

"Are you sure he wasn't trying to get around to saying I am the one in darkness?"

"My, aren't we paranoid!" Myra said.

Jaynie waved tentatively then walked away.

"Anyway, if he was trying to do that, no one bit," Liia said. "I heard about your epic walk this morning. How are the toes?"

"They're sore. I should have listened to Myra's wisdom."

"They'll heal, and you made a statement. I think that's more important than saving toes," Liia said.

"Do we have to try to bring light to Willow, too?" slithered through the air. I froze with a mixture of guilt and anger.

"Shut up, John," Myra barked. "Just consider the source, Willow. Don't pay him any attention."

"Who is that idiot?" Liia asked.

"It's John the jerk," Myra said. "He's just a ratty little sophomore."

"It still hurts, even if the source is questionable," I managed.

"Let's do this light thing," Myra said and gave me a hug.

"My turn." Liia hugged me tightly. "I know it's hard, but try to let the nastiness roll off."

I willed the tears to stay put. "Thanks. I'm glad you moved here," I said, holding onto the hug.

"Hey, do you want a piggyback ride to the car?" Will called from across the room.

"What's wrong with your feet?" I jumped, not realizing Roger had come up behind me. "Sorry to startle you, but I noticed you were limping when you came in."

"I have blisters on both feet from walking in my heels."

"Sorry about that. I noticed you haven't signed up for a position for Youth Sunday."

"I signed up twice," I said, muscles tightening.

"Well… we still need another greeter."

My arm was pulled while I glared at Roger. "We need to get going. Supper will be waiting, you know." It was Will.

I resisted for a second and then let his pull move me away. Myra and Liia came along behind us.

"What was that about?" Myra asked when we got to the parking lot.

"We had a plan that if Willow started to lose it, I was to drag her out of there. It worked perfectly," Will explained.

Myra and Liia laughed. "That was brilliant," Liia said.

"Hey, do y'all want to come over and hang out for a while?" I asked, feeling the need for some support.

"Thanks, but I have school work to do. It never ends," Myra responded.

"I'd love to," Liia said. "Let me check with the parents." She sent a text.

"One more week till Christmas break! I can't wait," Will said.

"Yay! And Christmas is just a week from Tuesday!" Myra added. "Will you go back to Sweden?"

"We're flying out Saturday morning. It will be nice to see my grandparents again."

"Aw. We'll miss you over the break," I said.

"Thanks."

"You have to send us pictures of Christmas in Sweden!" Myra requested, clapping her hands.

"Yeah, that's a great idea!" I echoed.

"I can do that. Maybe we could do a Facetime call, too."

"That would be fun," Myra said.

Liia's phone pinged. "They said I could go!"

"I'm off to study," Myra sighed. "Y'all have fun."

"Let's go. It's cold standing here," Will grumped.

"Mom, Dad, this is Liia. She's the girl from Sweden I've been telling you about," I said when we got to the house.

"Nice to meet you, Liia. I hope coming to America wasn't too much of a shock," Mom smiled.

"I'm adjusting well, thanks."

"You're making your famous ham soup. Is it OK if Liia stays for supper?"

"Of course."

"Come on. Let me show you my room." I dragged Liia down the hall. "I'm glad you came! It will help take some pressure off at supper. My parents won't grill me about being gay with you here. At least I hope!"

"Are they still doing that?"

Taz hopped onto the bed and sniffed Liia's hand. "This is Taz, my little buddy."

"Nice to meet you," Liia greeted Taz, stroking her back.

"I don't think they will ever be able to accept me. Let's talk about something less depressing, like your hair. How do you get the green highlights in?"

"I'd go to a salon in Sweden, and they would pull part of the hair through foil, just like you do any other highlights. I like to change colors for different seasons. I usually go red for Christmas, but I haven't found a salon here yet."

"I like the green. It accents your eyes," I said, noticing just how green Liia's eyes are. "I bet the lady who cuts my hair could do that for you. Her name is Lisa, and the shop is called Hair Dimensions. I think she does a great job."

"You do have a nice haircut. I'll have to try her. I'm going to see my hairdresser while I'm in Sweden, so it will be a while before I need her."

"I'd love to go to Sweden."

"Maybe you could go with us sometime. That would be fun!"

"Dinner time!" Mom called from the kitchen.

As we chit-chatted through supper, I noticed an odd feeling. I was genuinely happy. I hadn't felt that in a long time. No one was talking about my being gay. Things felt... normal.

After supper, I drove Liia home. "Thanks for coming over. That was fun."

"Thanks for having me. I had a great time."

I felt an urge to reach out and touch her but resisted. I watched her walk to the door, and she turned and waved. I waved back and drove home.

I spread out my calculus book and notebook on the bed. I tried to focus on homework but kept thinking back to Liia's visit.

Chapter 21

Tuesday, December 18, 2018

Pulling into the school parking lot, I checked my watch. 7:40. *Plenty of time!* I noticed Myra's car pulling in as I put on my backpack and hurried over.

"Did you get it done?" I asked.

"I did, but I was up till one o'clock."

"You'll be sleepy today."

"If I nod off during class, poke me," Myra laughed. "I'm glad that paper is done. It's a big weight off my shoulders."

"I'm sure it's great, even if you were half-asleep while writing it."

We walked to our lockers. I noticed something on the front of mine long before we got there. "What's that stuck on my locker?"

"Maybe someone left you a love note."

When I was close enough to see it, my blood chilled and my hand flew to my mouth.

Myra gasped. "That's horrible! We have to tell someone!" She took a photo with her phone and left me frozen in place.

I pulled off the paper and stared. It was a mallet and wooden stake drawn in black ink. Blood dripped from the stake. My hands shook so it was hard to see the details. I forced them to be still so I could read the words at the bottom.

"Repent or Die in your Sin!" More blood dripped from the word, "Sin." Numbness crept up my arms. I couldn't stop staring at it. I jumped when Myra touched my shoulder.

"This was taped on Willow's locker this morning." The words sounded far off.

"May I see that?" It was Ms. Price. She was holding out her hand. I couldn't seem to move my hand to give it to her. I did manage to nod my head.

"That's disgusting. I hope this is just a mean prank, but we need to take precautions. May I take this to Dr. Taylor?"

My voice wouldn't work. I nodded my head.

"I think you need to come with me," Ms. Price said.

"You don't look so good. Are you OK?" Myra asked. When I didn't answer, Myra took my arm and tugged. "Come on. I'll walk with you.

My feet moved at Myra's prodding. My stomach turned queasy and everything seemed a blur as we walked to the office.

"Dr. Taylor, these girls found this on Willow's locker this morning. It seems like a serious threat." She handed the note over.

I watched as Dr. Taylor's brow creased. Her face hardened. "You're right. We can't allow threats like this in our school. I'll get the police involved. We'll have to go over the security video."

She looked up from the note. "I need to keep this for the police. You girls go on to class."

I felt like I returned to my body. The shock was easing. "Who would have done that?" I asked when we were out in the hall.

"I don't know, but they are sick," Myra said.

"I'm glad you were with me. I wish I had never told Ben. I can't believe he turned on me." My shock shifted toward rage. "I need to give him a piece of my mind." I was stomping down the hall.

"Hold on a minute," Myra said, catching my arm and pulling me to a stop. "This was not Ben's doing. This is someone with a really warped brain."

"You're right, as usual. I just want to make someone pay for this. It's not fair. It's not right!"

The hall was filling with students on their way to class. I studied each face, wondering who was responsible.

"Do you think you need to go home?" Myra asked.

"Why would you say that? No. I don't need to go home. No. I'm not going to let them run me off."

"OK. Let's get to class before we're late."

I tried to focus on what Mr. Carlisle was teaching, but my mind kept wandering back to the horrible picture. *Why would someone want to threaten my life? Who would do that?*

"Willow?" filtered into my consciousness. "Are you with us?" It was Mr. Carlisle.

"She's had a traumatic morning," Myra said. "Someone put a threatening note on her locker."

"I see," Mr. Carlisle said. "Please try to focus, Willow."

"I'll be happy to work the problem," Liia said.

My cheeks blushed when I realized Mr. Carlisle had called me to the board. Liia walked up and worked the problem perfectly.

"That's exactly right," Mr. Carlisle beamed. "Does everyone understand how she did that?" Heads nodded. I smiled at Liia as she walked back to her seat. "Good job," I whispered and gave her a thumbs up. "Thanks for rescuing me!"

"You're welcome," she mouthed as she sat down.

Some of the shattered pieces of my heart knitted back together with Liia's kind gesture.

"You have the last ten minutes of the period to get started on tonight's homework."

I forgot to write down the assignment. I scolded myself. I copied it down and tried to focus on the first problem. The numbers sat on the page mocking me. I checked, and Liia was writing furiously. *I really like her.*

I had gotten nowhere when the bell rang. I was packing my books when I felt a warm touch on my shoulder.

"Just checking to see if you're OK," Liia inquired.

"Is it that obvious?"

"Mr. Carlisle called on you three times."

"Wow!"

Liia laughed.

"Someone left a disgusting note on her locker," Myra said, joining the conversation.

"What was it?"

"A mallet and a stake, with blood dripping off the stake," I said. I couldn't bring myself to mention the words at the bottom.

"Like they use to kill vampires?" Liia asked.

"I guess so." I felt even more stricken.

During second period, "Please send Willow to the office," sounded over the intercom. The class gave the expected ooohs of shame that usually followed such an announcement.

I caught the concerned look on Liia's face. "I'm not in trouble," I mouthed and left the class.

The secretary directed me into Dr. Taylor's office. The school resource officer and my parents were already there.

"Are you OK?" Mom asked as I walked in.

"I am a little shaken," I replied, feeling even more unsettled seeing my parents there.

"Is this Willow?" the officer asked, standing with erect military posture. He was a fit looking thirty-seven year old with wavy red hair.

"I am."

"Willow, this is officer Benefield. He is helping to investigate the note that was left on your locker," Dr. Taylor clarified.

"Thank you," I said.

"I checked the surveillance footage. There were three people involved. Unfortunately they were all wearing hoods and ski masks, so I am not able to identify them. Based on their physiques, I am fairly sure they are all male. But that doesn't give us much to go on."

"Do you think my daughter is in danger?" Dad asked.

"Usually this sort of thing is a prank, but the gruesome nature of the picture is concerning."

"What should we do?" Mom asked.

"I advise being cautious," Officer Benefield said. "Don't go anywhere that you will be alone. Stay with friends. If you see someone suspicious lurking around a restroom or in the parking lot, turn and go back. That sort of thing."

"Officer Benefield will be on alert, and I'll make the staff aware of what has happened. We will do everything we can to keep you safe, so try not to worry," Dr. Taylor said. "We will not tolerate this kind of behavior in our school."

"Thank you so much," Mom said. "Willow, do you want us to check you out for the rest of the day?"

I was surprised by her question and thought before answering. *I want to say, "Yes," and get away. I want to run and never come back. But I can't do that. I have to stay.* Something inside stirred, and I felt my spine stiffen. "No, I'm not checking out. I'm not going to let whoever did this run me off. I'm going to stay and fight."

I saw pleading in my parents eyes as they looked to Dr. Taylor.

"You know we can't allow fighting in the school," Dr. Taylor said.

"That's not what I meant. I meant that I am not going to let someone this petty beat me."

"Are you sure you don't have an idea who did this?" Dr. Taylor asked. "I think it would be best to ignore it rather than to confront them if you do."

"I agree," Officer Benefield said. "The best thing you can do for yourself is to ignore them and go on with your life. Don't ask anyone if they know who did it. Just pretend that it didn't happen. That's also the worst thing you can do to the perpetrators. It will render there aggression pointless if you ignore them," he finished with a wink.

"Do you think you can do that for us?" Dr. Taylor asked.

I wanted to find someone and beat them up. My fear had morphed into rage, but I sensed the wisdom in Officer Benefield's words. "I'll try my best to do just that."

"Great," Dr. Taylor said. "Remember to be careful in restrooms, too. I'll have a couple of teachers posted in the parking lot for a few days. I believe your safest place is here, inside the school."

"Thank you for taking the extra measures to protect my daughter," Dad said.

"You are quite welcome. We take the safety of our students very seriously," Dr. Taylor responded.

"We don't agree with the lifestyle she wants to choose, but we do want her safe," Dad added.

My rage flared. I clenched my teeth to keep from exploding at Dad. A palpable silence filled the room. *Did everyone else see the crassness of his comment?... Or did they agree with him?* Finally I said, "May I go back to class now?"

"Anything else?" Dr. Taylor asked, looking around the room. No one said anything, so she continued, "Yes, go on back to class. Please let me know if anyone taunts you or threatens you."

"Thanks." I got out of the office as quickly as I could.

Chapter 22

Tuesday, December 18, 2018

The moment I sat down in class after returning from the office, the bell rang. "How did it go? Liia asked.

"They said they can't identify the people from security videos, so they told me to be careful."

"Why can't they identify the creep?"

"They were wearing ski masks. There were three of them, the officer said."

"Do you think it could be a gang?"

A chill ran down my spine. "Gee thanks! I hadn't thought of that. I don't even know if we have gangs in this school."

I settled into my desk for English composition with my mind still reeling from Liia's comment. I tried to focus on what Ms. Price was saying. It was something about topic sentences and paragraph development. *I don't want to be a target of gang activity. The ugliness of the picture makes it seem possible, though.*

I tuned back in long enough to hear, "Your assignment is to write a three paragraph essay on a topic of your choice. I want you to pay serious attention to the topic sentences."

I was staring at the brown hat with three feathers Ms. Price was wearing. It suited her dark features and added flair to her outfit. It was a nice reprieve from thinking about the note.

I have to come up with a topic. My mind was spinning, settling on nothing. I was still looking at the hat. *I have no idea where I'm going but let me try this.* I wrote my first sentence, "A hat with feathers lightens the heart."

It's silly, but I have to write something! I went on to describe the hat in the first paragraph, used the second to tell how it lightened my day, and summarized in the third. In parentheses at the bottom of the page, I added, "Thanks for the inspiration!"

"I hope you didn't write about that note!" Myra said on our way out.

"Nope. I wrote about Ms. Price's hat."

"You didn't!"

"I did. It was the only thing I could think of, and it actually made me feel better."

Myra laughed. "You're nuts!"

"What did you write about?"

"How plastics are affecting the planet."

"That sounds like you."

My nerves were tight at the end of the day. I stepped out of the building and scanned the parking lot, frightened of the walk to my car. Something touched my elbow, and my feet left the ground.

"Sorry! I didn't mean to startle you," Myra said.

"I'm a little on edge."

"I'd say. Well, I'm walking you to your car."

"Me, too!" Liia's cheerful voice sounded.

"Thanks. I see Mr. Carlisle is stationed at the next door."

"We've got this. Let's go," Myra said, taking my elbow. Liia took the other, and we headed toward my car. I started laughing.

"What's so funny," Liia asked.

"I'm picturing the scene in the Wizard of Oz where Dorothy, the Lion, and the Tin Man take off arm in arm." We all laughed.

Will came running up. "I heard about the note! That was terrible."

"How did you hear about it?"

"What do you mean? The whole school knows by now."

"It was nerve rattling."

"I guess tennis is off for today."

"Are you crazy? I need something to burn off this nervous energy. I'll race you to the courts!" The day was just starting to take on some normalcy. I froze as I rounded the back of my Jeep. My hand flew to my mouth to stifle a scream.

"What's wrong," Liia asked. "Oh, no!"

"Mr. Carlisle!" Myra called. He didn't seem to hear, so she took off running. "Mr. Carlisle! We need you!"

I stared at the back window. My hands were shaking. Painted on the window was the same mallet and stake. Underneath was the word, "Condemned."

Will and Liia wrapped their arms around me. "This is just sick," Will said.

Myra came charging back with Mr. Carlisle in tow. "Look what they did to her car!"

I watched Mr. Carlisle's face scrunch up. He pulled out his phone and took several photos. "This has gone from prank to serious. I assume you just found this?"

My voice had been stolen again, so I nodded. Mr. Carlisle dialed. "Hey, Dr. Taylor. We just found the same image on the back of Willow's car. Can you get Todd over here?"

He listened "That's right. I think this is urgent. Can we get someone to take over directing traffic for him? I don't want to leave Willow alone here."

Another pause. "Yes, I think it's that serious." I saw the corner of his mouth drop as he hung up.

"What did she say?" Myra asked.

"She's going to get Officer Benefield to come look at this."

My heart was racing, and I tried to will it to slow down. I pulled away from Will and Liia and reached to touch the image.

"Wait, don't touch that," Will said. "The police need to see it first."

"I just want to see if it's still wet." My finger was poised in midair.

"Will's right. They may want to dust for fingerprints," Mr. Carlisle added.

"I can't imagine why anyone would do something this horrible just because she is gay," Liia said. "This kind of thing doesn't happen in Sweden."

I saw Mr. Carlisle's eyes widen a bit. "Do you think that is what this is about?" He seemed genuinely surprised.

"Probably," Myra said.

Time moved like a worm crawling uphill as we waited for Officer Benefield to come. Mr. Carlisle kept glancing at me. I wondered if I had grown a unicorn horn. *I have to do something to deflect this scrutiny.* "Y'all can go if you need to. I can wait for Officer Benefield."

"Honey, I'm not going anywhere," Myra answered. "You don't need to face this alone."

"I agree," Will and Liia said at the same time.

I watched Officer Benefield walk quickly across the parking lot, concern etched on his face.

"Oh," he said as he studied the image with its caption. "This has gone from prank to assault." He took a few pictures with his phone. "It's time to call in an investigator." He dialed the precinct.

"This is Officer Benefield, SRO for Hawksville High. We have a case of vandalism and assault on campus and need an investigator pronto. I sent in a photo… Roger that and thank you."

He pocketed the phone. "Now, tell me everything that happened. I'm assuming this is your car, Willow, so you start, please."

"Myra and Liia walked me to my car. Will joined us. I was walking around the back of the car when I saw it."

"Did you see anyone around your car?"

"No, but there were a lot of students in the parking lot."

"Did any of you notice anything suspicious?"

"No, I think it was done before we left the building," Myra said.

"I'll check the surveillance footage, but I bet they were masked again."

Anxiety hit hard. I wanted to run and hide. The parking lot felt so open, so exposed. I scanned the parking lot, not sure what I was looking for. Everything seemed normal, a steady stream of cars leaving. My eyes were drawn to a dark figure moving quickly. I didn't comprehend what I was seeing at first. He seemed in a rush to get into the car.

"There!" I shouted. "In the blue Mustang! He's wearing a dark hood like the people in the video!" I started to run toward the car, but Will stopped me.

"Are you crazy? There's no telling what the guy might do if you caught him."

Officer Benefield was snapping pictures. Then he tried to run the car down. It was moving too fast and exited the parking lot before he could catch it.

I watched him study his phone as he walked back.

"Good, I got the license plate. We will definitely have a talk with this person." He wasn't even out of breath after his dash.

I shivered as the wind picked up. It was a cloudy, dreary day.

"Whew! It's cold out here. I'm going to need you to stick around until the investigator is done. Why don't you wait in the office? Would one of you wait with her?" Officer Benefield scanned their faces.

"I will," three voices said together. We laughed, and they escorted me back to the building.

Halfway there, Liia said, "Oh no! I forgot to tell Dad not to come yet." We saw his car turn off the road. "I'm sorry, but I'll have to go."

"That's OK. Thanks for staying as long as you did."

She leaned in and hugged me. "Please stay safe." I willed the tears to stay put.

"We'll make sure nothing happens to her," Will said.

Chapter 23

Mary Hollister, the secretary, waved to us through the office door, beckoning us in. *She was expecting us.* She pushed back her salt and pepper hair and said, "Please have a seat. Willow, your mom will be here soon. I'm so sorry this is happening."

"Thanks. It's turning into a nightmare." She slid her reading glasses back on and returned her focus to the computer.

We sat down, Will on one side and Myra on the other. Mary's taps on the keyboard filled the silence. A pleasant feeling worked through my soul. *Safe. I'm nestled between two people who will love me no matter what. How can some people be so nice and supportive while others are so cruel? Why does my being gay stir up so much hatred? I'm the same person I've always been. Nothing has really changed except that I have more clarity on who I am. I haven't done anything to these people, so why are they attacking me?*

The printer growled to life, and I jumped. Mary smiled and said, "Sorry, it's just the printer."

"My nerves are a little wired."

"That's understandable," she said and went back to her work. As soon as the printer stopped she took the stack of papers and announced, "I'll be back in a bit."

"A penny for your thoughts," Myra said.

"I was just wondering how some people can be so nice and some so horrible. What did I ever do to these people? Just because they found out I'm gay, they think they have the God-given right to abuse me. I'd like for someone to show me where the Bible says we are supposed to abuse our neighbors as we wish!" My voice had hit a crescendo.

"Calm down," Will said, patting my leg.

"That's easy for you to say!"

"I know you're mad, but you don't want to raise the wrath of Dr. Taylor," he whispered.

I sighed.

"You're right though," Myra said. "The messages do make it sound like this is a religious thing. I think they are using a different Bible than the one I read."

"You said there were three of them on the video, right?" Will asked.

"That's what Officer Benefield said."

"Do you think it could be the stooges from youth group?"

"I can't believe John and Wyatt would do this," Myra said. "Besides, there are only two of them."

"But Billy is their buddy, too," Will observed. "We'll have to tell Officer Benefield about them."

The office door flew open and Mom rushed in, eyes narrowed. She squatted in front of me. "Are you OK? I saw the car! That note is pure evil! Who could be doing this?" Every word was coated in concern, and I felt buoyed by her care.

"I'm fine, and I have no idea who could be behind this. Two guys from the youth group have been harassing me, but I don't think they would stoop this low."

"I just want you to be safe! This is terrifying," Mom said as she squeezed me in a hug.

Officer Benefield entered, followed by a woman in a smart black business suit that accentuated her ebony skin and raven hair. "This is Detective Susan Godfrey. She'll be handling this case."

Detective Godfrey held out a hand. "Nice to meet you," she said, going around to each of us. "I'm guessing you are the victim and this is your mom," she directed to me.

"I'm Willow," I said, shaking her hand. *I've never thought of myself as a victim.*

She looked at Will and waited. Will caught on and said, "I'm Will, Willow's twin brother."

"And I'm Myra, Willow's friend."

"Great. I need a place where we can talk, just Willow and her mom," Detective Godfrey said.

She's all business. And she seems sharp.

"I think it's best if we conduct the interview in Dr. Taylor's office," Officer Benefield said.

"Principal?" Detective Godfrey asked.

"Yes," Officer Benefield said as he knocked on Dr. Taylor's door.

"Come in," sounded from within.

"Come with me, please," Detective Godfrey said, gesturing to Mom and me. "Would you two mind waiting in case I have some questions for you?"

Will and Myra nodded their heads.

"Hi, I'm Dr. Taylor, the school principal," she said, standing to shake Detective Godfrey's hand.

"Detective Godfrey, ma'am. I'll be handling this case."

"It's nice to meet you. Let's start with having Officer Benefield inform us as to what he has found so far.

"Sure. Willow and her friends stated that they noticed nothing unusual while walking out to the car. She did spot a person in a dark hoodie getting into a car. I tried to catch him, but only got a photo of the license plate. I think we should consider him a person of interest. I haven't checked the surveillance footage, but I suspect it will be the same perpetrators we saw at the locker," he explained.

"I would like to view the footage with you. I'll request a fingerprint team to dust the car and locker. I consider this a criminal threat, so we will do our best to catch the culprits," Detective Godfrey said. "In the meantime, I recommend taking extra precautions. Normally, I wouldn't be too concerned about this kind of thing, but the violent nature of the image is disturbing. What did you say the message on the note was?"

"Repent or die in your sin!" I said, the hair on the back of my neck standing at remembering the note.

"So this sounds like a religiously motivated attack. That doesn't mean it won't turn violent. I suggest you have a friend or teacher with you at all times. Don't go anywhere alone, even off campus, till we catch these guys," Detective Godfrey added.

"Oh, Will wanted me to tell you about two guys at church who have been harassing me."

"Good. That's another lead. Who are they?" she asked, pulling out a note pad.

"John Jackson and Wyatt Wilson," I answered with a twinge of guilt like I was tattling.

Detective Godfrey wrote down the names. "Can you give me a description?"

I started to describe John when Dr. Taylor interrupted. "Excuse me, but we can provide you with pictures, height and weight from our records."

"Perfect," she said. "Willow, do you know of anyone else who could potentially be behind this?"

I shook my head before I remembered. "Will said that Billy Baggett is a close friend of theirs. He might be the third one.

Detective Godfrey wrote that down then looked around the room, "Anyone else have anything to add?"

I watched the somber faces in the silence. Finally Mom asked, "Should we pull our daughter out of school till these people are caught?"

"No, I don't believe that is necessary," Detective Godfrey said. "Just take the precautions I recommended. The perpetrators know your locker, so they probably know your schedule as well. Bathrooms and empty hallways are prime places for attacks. I recommend having a teacher or friend go into the restroom ahead of you to make sure no one is lurking."

Great! I can't wait to have someone go to the bathroom with me. I don't want to announce that I need a teacher to hold my hand while I go! I didn't realize that I was hyperventilating until Mom asked, "Honey, are you OK?"

"I think all of this pressure is getting to me."

"I'm sorry. There *is* one thing that would make all of this go away."

The anger hit so hard that my stomach flipped, and I felt nauseated. "I can't believe you said that!" With fists clinched, I stormed out of the room.

Chapter 24

Sleep fought to stay away last night. Supper had been a tense affair. When my parents said that I could stop all of these problems by giving up this "crusade" going back to being "normal," Will said, "Someone is threatening to kill her, and you're only concern is about her sexuality!" That got him sent to his room. He is one of my anchors. In protest, I left the table and went to my room.

I was alone, but the conversation wouldn't stop. Like a never-ending parade, their statements about how I should give up my crusade and go back to being a normal person kept marching through. Each time the word, "crusade," passed, my blood boiled a little harder.

Then I would sink back into doubt, like quicksand slowly trying to swallow me. *Am I really just trying to join a cool fad?*

A wave of guilt would come through. *I am disappointing my parents. I should be better than that.* Anger would return with that thought. *No! I have to be true to myself. This is who I am!* Someone somewhere would press repeat, and it all started over.

The alarm sounded. I hit snooze and crawled back into bed. It didn't help. My mind continued to grind, and my eyes wouldn't shut. After three minutes I gave up and got up. I checked the weather before picking out what to wear.

Cloudy with a sixty percent chance of rain. High forty-nine. That's fitting. I dragged my gray mood around while I got ready for school. When I remembered my counseling appointment with Ms. Simpson was today, I brightened a bit.

I presented my note about the counseling appointment to Ms. Price.

"I see," she said. "Just a minute before you go. I read your essay from yesterday. So you like my hat?"

"I do. And with all that happened yesterday, I couldn't think of anything else to write about."

"I heard about the note. Good luck with your appointment. I'll catch you up when you get back."

"Thanks," and with that I was off to Ms. Simpson's office.

"Good morning," Ms. Simpson chirped, a bright smile lighting her face. She adjusted her glasses and said, "Have a seat."

I did my best to return the smile as I sat down. My lips stubbornly resisted.

"You seem weighed down," she said.

"Is it that obvious?"

"I'm afraid so."

"Yesterday was hard."

"I heard about the attacks. Tell me how you felt."

"It seems everyone has heard. I didn't sleep much last night worrying about all of this. I ended up feeling worse about my parents accusing me of just joining the latest fad than about the notes on my locker and car. They said I was on a crusade. I feel like I'm letting them down." I wiped away the tear worming its way out of the corner of my eye.

"It's hard when those we are closest to don't understand us. I'm not surprised that is more painful than a threat from someone you don't know. Tell me more about those feelings."

Pictures of my parents' scowling faces popped into my mind. The worming tear morphed into a flowing river, and I sobbed.

Between gushes, I managed to squeak out, "It…. hurts…. so…. bad."

Ms. Simpson was silent, waiting. I moved my hands away from my eyes long enough to see compassion on her face. I felt safe with her at that moment and knew I had made the right choice for a counselor. That realization seemed to dam up the tears, and I began to regain control. *All of these heavy emotions are irritating.*

I looked up at her. She waited. I didn't know what to say at that point.

"Sometimes a good cry is the best medicine," she said. "I have a couple of words of advice."

That's exactly what I need right now.

"First, you will have to be patient and give your parents time. This is a big change for them, particularly with their religious views. It's going to take some adjusting."

"I'm not sure they are going to adjust. They seem pretty adamant."

"Patience is hard. The second thing is that your parents' difficulty in accepting your sexual orientation is not your fault. It's their problem."

"It sure feels like my problem. I'm the one suffering for it." A twinge of anger flared.

"You have to trust that they are hurting, too. You are their precious daughter, and they want what is best for you."

I held my tongue, trying to decide if she was right or if I needed to fight. *Maybe she's right.* "OK, I'll try to be patient and give them the benefit of the doubt," I finally answered.

"Good. Now let's shift gears and talk about the messages on your locker and car."

Memory of the fear I felt yesterday crashed into my heart. I had managed to squelch that with the pain of my parents' rejection. Apparently it was ready and willing to come back.

"Tell me how you felt when you first saw the note on your locker."

"It was scary. I just froze and seemed to go numb. I'm glad Myra was there to take charge."

"It sounds like you were in shock."

"That's a good word for it."

"Did you feel any different when you saw the car?"

I considered that a moment. "It was a little less intense, but the same feeling of shock. I just don't understand why anyone feels the need to attack another person for something that's none of their business." The shock was turning to anger. I noticed my right hand was clenched into a fist. Apparently Ms. Simpson noticed it, too.

"People take their beliefs very seriously. Unfortunately, some think their personal beliefs should control how everyone else behaves, too. What did you make of the word 'condemned' that was on your car?"

I considered her question. An answer didn't come immediately. There seemed to be a swirl of emotion around that, but I couldn't find words to express it. I glanced at Ms. Simpson. She seemed willing to wait, so I delved back into the mess churning in my soul. Words began to emerge from the swirl. I spoke them as they came.

"Hurt. Afraid. Angry. That is my Jeep. How dare they defile it! Does God really condemn me? I was always taught that God loves us no matter what."

I looked, hoping Ms. Simpson would answer my question. She smiled gently.

"I can't presume to speak for God, but I don't think people who vandalize property and threaten another person could be considered reliable spokespersons either. You said you felt afraid. What are you afraid of?"

"That they are right." I said that so quickly it surprised me.

"That bothers you more than the fact that someone may be planning to do you harm?"

"I think so, since that's the first thing that came to mind."

"Have you considered talking with your pastor about this?"

"Our youth minister has already made it clear that he disapproves of homosexuality. He won't even let me participate in the service for Youth Sunday. I don't want to talk to him."

"How about the senior pastor?"

"I haven't considered that," I said slowly as I wondered what Pastor Stevens would think. *I really don't know her very well. She's an unknown.* "Sorry, I was lost in thought," I said when I realized Ms. Simpson was speaking.

"I was saying that the senior pastor might be able to help with your religious questions better than I."

She looked at the clock, and my heart sank. "I believe it is time for you to return to class. I'll look forward to seeing you next week."

"Thanks. These sessions are really helpful," I said, meaning it. I got up to leave.

"And Willow?"

"I turned and registered concern in her eyes. "Yes?"

"Please be careful. We don't know what these people will do next."

"OK." I walked out the door a little shaken. I wished her eyes hadn't said more than her words. *What if these people intend to hurt me? Oh well, I'll deal with that later.*

Chapter 25

I walked back to Ms. Price's room trying to shake the icky feeling that Ms. Simpson's expression had left me with. The bathroom was coming up, and it reminded me I needed to go. I knew I wasn't supposed to go alone, but I just couldn't bring myself to walk into the classroom and ask for someone to go with me. *Too much embarrassment.*

I paused by the door. *OK, I'll poke my head in. If there is anyone in there who looks threatening, I'll leave.* I peeked in and saw no one. I realized my heart was racing as I walked through the door. "I'm OK. I'm OK," I repeated, trying to calm down.

I did my business and was relieved to exit the bathroom. I almost missed seeing it when I opened Ms. Price's door, but it caught my eye when the door was halfway open. I froze, and the world went fuzzy except for the mallet and stake. This time the blood was red.

I heard sound, but it was muffled, like it was coming through water. Ms. Price was beside me, and her words finally registered. "Willow, come on…"

She stopped abruptly. I tore my eyes away from the paper to look at her. "Oh, no!" she said. She pulled me by the arm into the classroom and closed the door. I tripped over my toe once but caught myself. I heard a few snickers.

Then I heard, "Yes?" come over the intercom.

"We have another note," Ms. Price said.

"I'll send Officer Benefield."

I was still standing in front of the class. My cheeks flushed, and I went to my seat. It seemed an eternity before Ms. Price said, "OK class, please resume your writing assignment."

I scanned the board to try to figure out what the assignment was but didn't see anything. Then I heard someone running in the hall. "They're going to get in trouble," I thought. The running stopped at Ms. Price's door.

I wiped my sweaty palms on my jeans and waited. The door opened and Officer Benefield stepped through it.

"I'm sorry to disturb the class, but we have a threatening note posted on the door." He the door open so everyone could see. "Did anyone see who did this?"

I saw heads shaking all around the classroom.

"Did anyone hear a sound at the door during class?"

"I did hear something, but I thought it was the heat coming on and rattling the door," Ms. Price said.

"Did you notice the time?" Officer Benefield asked as he pulled out a notepad.

"I'd say it was ten to fifteen minutes after class started," she answered. "It was after Willow left for her appointment."

I would just as soon the attention turn away from me.

"Who found the note?"

"I did," I squeaked.

"I'm going to let Detective Godfrey know. She may want to speak to you when she gets here."

I sighed a little too loudly, and my cheeks flushed again. Officer Benefield left. Even with the door closed, I could still clearly see the word on the note: FORSAKEN.

Liia's hand was on my forearm. I put mine on top of hers and looked over. The concern in her eyes made me feel less forsaken.

The drill of being called to the office, talking about the incident and being told to be careful was getting too familiar. Mom was there and had given me a hug when I walked in. Her concern seemed genuine. *Maybe she is thawing.*

This time there was only one person on the surveillance footage, hoodie and ski mask in place. Mom offered to check me out, but I insisted on staying. I still refused to let these goats run me off.

Back in Mr. Spellman's class I realized I should have checked out. But it was too late now. The class was political science, and it was boring. I usually had trouble focusing, but today was even worse. The word forsaken kept bouncing around inside my head like a pinball.

I wrote, "FORSAKEN,' on my paper and stared at it like that would help. The more I stared the more it seemed like just random sounds with no meaning.

What does that even mean? Sure, I've lost a few friends along the way, but I have never been forsaken. Is Jaynie forsaking me now? Maybe they are talking about God. Will you forsake me? Please don't. I need you, Lord.

Sometimes I hear people talking about how we need to get prayer back into the schools. Clearly they don't realize the amount of prayer students do at their desks.

I jumped, thinking Mr. Spellman had called on me. The words, "I'm sorry," were almost out when I realized he was questioning another student. *Embarrassment barely averted!*

OK, I have to get my mind back into class. Olivia was saying something about the Senate. *I know there are places where the Bible says homosexuality is wrong.* That thought made my heart sink. *Lord, does that mean that you will turn away from me? Is the note on the door right?*

I started to feel nauseated again. My heart raced and my palms were sweating.

"Willow, are you OK?" registered in my mind. It was Mr. Spellman. He'd noticed.

"Not really," I said before thinking. "Could I go get a drink of water?" He eyed me suspiciously.

"Sure, give that a try."

I walked to the door and looked both ways like I was crossing the road before entering the hall. No one was there. I held to the water fountain a few seconds before taking three drinks. The cold wetness soothed my dry mouth and seemed to calm the fire growing in my gut. I took three more sips.

"Ooh, Willow's skipping class," hit my ears like a hammer, and I jumped. I hadn't heard anyone coming down the hall, but there were John and Wyatt.

"It looks like you are, too," I retorted, not as much a zinger as I wanted.

"Yeah. It's great!" Wyatt said, and they kept walking.

More water. If they are responsible for the notes, I think they would have said something about them. Maybe it wasn't them. I looked at my watch. School would be over in eleven minutes. *I think I can make that.* I went back to class.

Finally the bell rang. I packed my backpack and left the classroom. All of my friends had avoided political science, heeding its reputation for boredom. I had decided to go ahead and get it out of the way since it was required for college. I signed up as dual enrollment. If I could pass the final in a few days, I'd be done!

Quick footsteps registered in my ear amidst the buzz of the crowd. Someone was in a hurry. A tinge of fear zinged my spine just before someone grabbed me.

"Are you OK?"

I nearly jumped out of my skin. It was Liia. "I was till you just about scared the life out of me!" She hugged me tighter.

"Sorry about that. I heard about another note. This is getting too freaky."

"That it is. This time the blood was colored red."

She leaned her head next to mine, and the tension seemed to ooze out of me. I wrapped my arm around her and hugged her back. "Thanks for being my friend."

"I'm really glad we met. Now we have to keep these creeps from hurting you."

She took my arm, and I knew she was going with me all the way to my car. We had hardly started walking when another surprise hug zoomed in.

"I can't believe they did it again!" Myra said. "I hope they catch these jerks soon."

"Me, too," Liia and I said together.

Myra took my other arm as we marched to my car. I saw Jaynie coming toward me down the hall. She had an awkward expression, stopped, then turned and went the other way. My heart seemed three pounds heavier all of a sudden.

My whole body felt heavier as we approached my car. I dreaded what I might find. When we were close enough, I could tell that the back window was still clean. I'd washed it with Windex to get off any remaining crud from those creeps. I didn't relax till we had circled the car and had found no notes.

Myra waved and gave a thumbs up to Mr. Carlisle. "I think we need Bellini's to celebrate!"

"I think you are right," I said, relieved to do something normal.

Chapter 26

Wednesday, December 19, 2018

I looked up from saying the blessing, and my parents' tense expressions made me nervous. I didn't say anything and started eating, though I wasn't very hungry after the Bellini's yogurt earlier.

The tinkle of forks on plates seemed loud in the dense silence. I knew I should let the sleeping dog lie, but I just couldn't help it. "What?" I asked.

"We have something we want to talk to you about, Honey," Mom answered.

"OK," I sat up straighter wondering what was coming.

"We found a program that helps people like you," Dad said.

"What do you mean, 'people like me?'" I answered, making air quotes for emphasis. I should have kept my mouth shut, but I'm sure they would have brought it up anyway.

"It's a program that helps people who feel they are homosexual get back on the right path," Mom explained, raising her eyebrows in hope.

I dropped my fork, and it clanked onto the table. I looked at them as if they were green aliens.

"We would like you to go into the program after Christmas. It's a one to two-week stay," Dad said.

"A one to two week stay?" My voice sounded like a robot. I wasn't sure it was even mine. My fingers turned cold, and my hands were shaking. I put them under my legs to stop them.

"That's right, Honey. And from what we have read, they have a good success rate." *Mom sounds so far away.*

"It's a Christian program, and if you go in right after Christmas you won't miss any school. No one will even have to know."

That was Dad. My mind seemed to be filled with sludge. My heart was screaming, "Run!" but I couldn't seem to engage my mind. I needed to respond to this threat. I felt drugged. *Would they drug me to get me to say yes? Maybe to drag me to the place, but that would be next week. No, I don't think I'm drugged.*

Everything seemed to have gone dark. *Did the power go out? No, the light is on. Why is it so dark. They are staring at me!*

"Honey are you OK?" slid through the sludge. I wanted to slip into the sludge and never come out. It felt safer in there.

"Ridiculous." I heard the word, "Ridiculous." It was Will. His voice began to break through.

"First of all, there is nothing wrong with Willow that needs fixing. Secondly, those places are soul-crushing torture camps that try to beat heterosexual thinking into people who aren't heterosexual. The only reason they work is that when people come out they are terrified to admit their true identity again. You can't do that to Willow!"

He was shouting by the end. His volume seemed to push the sludge a little out of the way. I saw Dad's jaw clench. I expected Will to be sent to his room.

"I appreciate your taking up for your sister. I'm glad you do that, but I think your mother and I know what is best for her. Let's mull this over for a day and let the dust settle. We do have to let Sword of Grace know for sure by Friday, though," Dad said.

My mind found its connection to my voice. "I'm not going."

"Like I said," Dad growled, "Think it over tonight, and we'll talk about it tomorrow."

"Tomorrow won't change things. I am not going to a place like that. I am who God made me to be, and you want to change that? That's not very Christian of you!" I was raising my voice.

"I expect respect out of my children," Dad snarled, his nostrils flaring. I had gotten under his skin and was glad.

"Like Dad said, let's all just think about this, and we'll see what it looks like tomorrow," Mom added.

"It will look worse tomorrow!" I said. I slid my chair back and left the table without another word,

"But you haven't eaten your supper," followed me down the hall. I didn't respond. I hoped Will would follow me, but I knew he would have more trouble going without food. I slammed my door for effect.

Lying down on the bed, I expected to cry. Rage flowed in to replace the sludge instead of tears. *How dare they! I won't go. They will have to drug me to get me there. If they insist, I'll run away.*

That last thought scared me, but it seemed like a possible option. *Let's think more about this.* Taz rubbed her chin on my cheek and purred. She had long ago taken my room as her favorite spot to sleep, either on my bed or in the little bed that I kept next to my headboard.

"Do you want to come with me?" She meowed. "Don't agree too quickly. This may actually happen." She spun around in two circles and lay down next to my arm.

Where could I go? They would probably get the police after me since I'm only seventeen. I do need to finish school. Maybe running away isn't the answer.

Taz was purring. It made me wish I were a cat. Her life seemed so pleasant, the opposite of mine right now. I scratched her ear, and she put her paw against my hand to help me find just the right spot.

"Taz, I have more homework to do. You keep the bed warm, and I'll join you when I finish." I went to my desk and opened the calculus book. I was an oddity to my friends because I liked math *and* language arts. Most of them liked one or the other and despised the one they didn't like. I was looking forward to working the problems. It would get my mind off the nightmare brewing at the table.

Halfway through the first problem, my stomach rumbled. I was hungry but refused to give my parents the satisfaction of knowing that by going to the kitchen. The granola bar in my backpack would have to do. I tried to eat it slowly, hoping it would get me to bedtime.

I set pencil to paper, but my mind short circuited. It jumped back to the table nightmare. *Sword of Grace. That sounds terrifying! I need to find out about this place.*

I opened my web browser and typed in "Sword of Grace." Sure enough, there was a place with that horrible name. "It sounds like they plan to carve me into little pieces." That thought made me shiver. I didn't like this place already.

I clicked on the "About Us" tab. "Sword of Grace is a Bible-based ministry dedicated to shepherding teens and young adults who have wandered down an unbiblical path back to the narrow way that leads to salvation. We use time-honored psychological methods and intense immersion into biblical studies to achieve the goal of reforming people who have fallen into the traps of alternative lifestyles."

They can't even say the word homosexual! How could they possibly help me? Well, that's all I need to know about this place. It sounds like they plan to beat the gayness out of me. Life was a lot easier before I made this discovery about myself. But it was hollow. I never really felt at home in my skin till I opened this can of worms. Now I feel more at home inside, but there are nothing but tornadoes outside. Is it better to be at peace in my heart or to keep the peace outside? Why can't I have both, Lord?

That little prayer left me feeling sad. I knew my parents had already made up their minds that I was going to that awful sounding place. I had to make up my mind how far I would go to avoid it.

Chapter 27

Thursday, December 20, 2018

It was cold, and frost formed a gentle blanket over everything as I drove to school. Will had waited for me to get ready and was following right behind. I loved my twin brother, and I knew he loved me, which is why he insisted on walking with me into school.

I passed Myra's car on my way to my parking space and noticed that it was still running. *She just got here.* Myra was usually earlier than I was. I parked, pulled my backpack from the passenger seat and got out.

To my surprise, Myra and Liia were standing there with Will. Bright "Good mornings" warmed the cold air.

"Good morning to you, too!" I said. Looking into their concerned faces, I realized it wasn't *all* tornadoes outside. This little group was my safe harbor. They believed in me, and I was grateful.

"I am so thankful for you three. You just don't know how much it means that you care." I willed the budding tears to stop.

"We love you, too," Myra chirped and put her arm around my shoulders.

"I hope we don't find another note today," Liia said, taking my arm on the other side.

"We're off to see the wizard," Myra said and pulled me toward the school.

As we closed in on the door, my nerves tensed. *Where would it be today.* Will stayed with us all the way to my locker. "No note," I observed.

Will took off for his class, and the remaining three of us went to first period. My feet seemed to get heavy as we neared the door, slowing me down.

"Let me check," Myra said, appearing to have detected my apprehension.

"I hope this nightmare is over soon," Liia said.

"The nightmare is getting worse at home," I answered, feeling my stress level rise just thinking about it.

"All clear!" Myra reported and came back to where I had stopped.

"What's happening at home?" Liia asked, her eyes wide.

"Oh no. More drama?" Myra asked.

"Yeah, last night my parents announced they are going to put me into a facility that turns gay people back to straight."

"What!" both of them said.

"They said I had to go in right after Christmas."

"That's just sick!" Myra said.

"I'm sorry. I can't even imagine how awful that feels," Liia said. I could tell she was sincere.

"I told them I'm not going, and I'm not."

"You do realize that parents can pretty much do what they want to with us until we're eighteen," Myra said.

"I know. But the only way they will get me in that place is to drug me or have the police take me." My stress was morphing into anger, and I could hear my heartbeat.

"I've heard of parents calling the police to get their kids into a drug program," Myra said.

Myra was always so analytical and so right. It was irritating, and her answer made me feel cornered. "They can't do that if they can't find me."

"Willow, what do you mean?" Myra asked. Liia's eyes got a little wider. *She has pretty green eyes.*

"I mean I'm thinking about running away if they push this. They wanted me to think about it overnight. I guess they thought I would see the wisdom of their plan if I just gave it time. The place is called Sword of Grace, like that's not scary!"

Myra was waving her palm toward the floor, and it dawned on me how loudly I was talking. Mr. Carlisle poked his head out the door, "Please keep the volume down."

"Yes sir," Myra said before laughing. "You do need to tone it down a bit. I think most of the school heard that," she said with her signature grin.

"Sword of Grace? That does sound awful," Liia added.

Her comment sealed my resolve not to go there, no matter what. "Well, I'm not going, and that's that."

"What are you going to tell your parents?" Myra asked.

"I'm going to tell them that I disagree with the program, that anything called Sword of Grace can't be good, and that I'm not going."

"Then what?" Myra asked. She was always the planner.

"Then, if they don't back down, I'll figure out the next step," I said, being more a fly by the seat of my pants kind of person.

"You could stay at my place if you need to. I'm sure I could convince my parents," Liia offered.

Where did this tear come from. I tried to force it back in, but there was another one right behind it. They squished out onto my cheeks. I wiped them and said, "Thank you."

"You're welcome," Liia said.

"Group hug!" Myra announced. "We've got your back."

The hug shored up my heart, but seemed to make the tears flow faster. "OK. I have to pull it together to go to class."

"Deep breaths. Now think of something funny," Myra directed.

I took three deep breaths. "I can't think of anything funny."

"How about three purple chickens singing 'Yankee Doodle Dandy?" Myra suggested.

It took a second, then all three of us burst into laughter.

"You're absolutely loony, Myra," I managed. We walked into class with the smiles still on our faces. Mr. Carlisle raised an eyebrow at us but didn't say anything.

I pulled out my notebook and calculus book before sitting down. Then I saw it. A piece of paper was just inside the opening underneath the desk top. My breath caught. I must have made a sound because everyone was looking at me. I pulled it out.

Everything seemed to be happening in slow motion. Sounds were muffled. I stared at the picture. I heard sounds but couldn't tell what they were. Mr. Carlisle's voice finally broke through. "We need officer Benefield in my room immediately."

The picture was the same mallet and stake. The red blood dripped into flames. *This person is a good artist,* ran through my mind. Then a wave of nausea hit. I started to bolt for the bathroom, but it subsided.

Officer Benefield rushed through the door. "Willow found another note," Mr. Carlisle explained.

Officer Benefield's eyes narrowed with concern as he walked to my desk. "Where did you find this?"

"It was in the desk."

"I see. Please put it back like you found it."

I put it back in the desk and looked at him.

"I need to take some photos."

I stepped away from the desk. After a few photos with his phone, he donned gloves and picked up the note. "I'm sure Detective Godfrey will want to talk to you again when she gets here, so be expecting a call to the office."

I nodded my head. Words refused to come just yet. I think Mr. Carlisle told me he was sorry this was happening before starting class.

The day slugged along. I was nervous waiting for the call to the office. It came during third period. Before I could get there, I heard my dad's voice. "This is a school! You have teachers everywhere! Why can't you catch these hoodlums who are threatening my daughter!"

As I opened the door, I heard, "We may have to put her in a private school if you can't protect her!"

I stood at Dr. Taylor's open door. "Come in, Willow," she said. Detective Godfrey and Officer Benefield were also there.

"I'm sorry we haven't been able to catch them yet. So far they have eluded us and seem to know just when no one will be on the hall where they leave the notes. I assure you that we have every staff member on the lookout for the culprits," Dr. Taylor said to my father, not even looking at me.

To be honest, right now I was more concerned about Sword of Grace and my dad's comment about private school. Neither appealed to me. I came out of my thoughts to discover the four adults looking at me. *Did someone ask me a question?* I just waited.

Detective Godfrey spoke. "We found no prints on the note, which is consistent with the previous ones. I am even more convinced the attacks are religiously motivated.

"We did check on the person you identified pulling out of the parking lot. He couldn't have been involved because he was getting help from a teacher when that first note was left. And we found him exiting the school and going straight to his car that afternoon. I will be interviewing the other two students you named today."

I liked her and felt I could trust her. She was all business but seemed genuine. "Thanks for your help."

"I think I already know the answer, but did you notice anyone or anything that might help us with this latest attack?" she asked.

"No. My friends and I walked into the classroom, and I found the note in my desk. Mr. Carlisle seemed shocked that someone had been able to get into his room to do that."

"OK, we will go through the drill of reviewing security footage and all that. At least we have two students to interview. Todd, would you mind setting up the security footage replays?"

"I'll be happy to."

They left the office leaving Dr. Taylor, Dad, and me. There was an awkward silence. "Can I go back to class?" *I would just as soon get out of here.*

"Yes, you may," Dr. Taylor said.

"I'll see you this afternoon. I'm going to have a few words with Dr. Taylor," Dad said.

I left with a heavy feeling that my future hung on those few words.

Chapter 28

Thursday, December 20, 2018

I was fuming. I would have spit molten lava at my dad had he been there. "Private school! I can't believe he was talking about putting me in a private school! I only have five months left till graduation!"

That was my second eruption of the afternoon. The first one had been while walking out of school with Myra and Liia. This time it was with Will on the tennis court.

"He was probably bluffing to try to get Dr. Taylor to take these attacks more seriously. It's hard to believe they haven't caught anyone yet."

"That's what Myra said. I hope y'all are right."

It was a gray cold day. The temperature was in the forties and the wind was blowing. I kept hitting the ball too hard and knocking it out of bounds.

After a few more volleys, Will said, "Maybe we should call it a day."

"Sorry, my mind is not on the game."

"You are a bit heavy-handed. Are you picturing Dad's face on the tennis ball?"

I laughed so hard I couldn't stand up straight. Will was always good at lightening the mood. When I finally regained control, I said, "Thanks, Will. I needed that."

"That's what wonderful brothers are for."

We went home. I wasn't sweaty, but I showered anyway. The hot water felt good and helped warm me up. I convinced myself that Will and Myra were right and that Dad wasn't really considering moving me to a private school. I hustled to get busy studying for my calculus final tomorrow.

The next thing I knew, Mom was calling us to supper. I scooted Taz off my lap, laid the pencil down in a careful diagonal, and went to the table.

"One more day till Christmas break!" Will said as we sat down to eat.

"I have to survive my calculus final," I said. I was dreading the test. I knew I could pass it, but I wanted to ace it.

"I'm worried about your going to school tomorrow. Those pictures keep getting uglier," Mom said.

"Yeah, I wish they would stop," I replied, wishing we could have one dinner without focusing on my issues. "Let's just not talk about that tonight. I need a break."

"I think we have to talk about it. I told Dr. Taylor that we are considering a private school for you next semester if they can't catch these creeps," Dad said.

"I'm not changing schools," I growled. My blood seemed to instantly boil. "That's just crazy. I am finishing these last five months with my friends and the teachers I know. Besides, if I change schools, the creeps win."

"It's not just that," he continued. "I think there are… influences in Hawksville High that are leading you down the wrong path. After your treatment at Sword of Grace, I think a fresh start would be best."

My blood went from boiling to vaporized. "About that," I said, trying to control my volume and tone. My voice was shaking with rage. "I have thought about this Sword of Grace idea, and I want you to know that I won't be going there." My throat dried up and stuck together. I had an explanation for why I wouldn't be going but couldn't get it out. I reached for a drink of tea to see if that would help. The silence felt as thick as my tongue.

"I had hoped the idea would grow on you as you thought about it," Dad said. I could tell by his face he had prepared for this fight.

"Honey, we just want what's best for you. You can see the problems you are already having from this… change," Mom said. "You are already losing friends. These nasty attacks at school keep happening. It's scary."

"You're just embarrassed that you have a homosexual daughter," I blurted out. I'm not sure where that came from, but it seemed to hit home.

"You are right. We are embarrassed that our daughter is going against the teaching of the church. It's not right. You have been taught better than that and yet you want to flaunt this… this immoral lifestyle in God's face."

"As far as I know, God says we are loved no matter what. Paul said nothing can separate us from the love of God, and I believe him!" My voice kept getting louder.

"Wow! You sound like a preacher!" Will said.

My brain was in fight mode. I looked at Will trying to comprehend what he said. When it registered I burst out laughing, and Will joined in.

Dad gave Will the death stare. "So you think this is funny? Well, it's not. This is serious. Willow is trying to ruin her life. We have to stop her and get her back on the right path."

I could see the vein near his temple pulsing with his heart beat. That's how I always could tell Dad was really angry. I would usually back down when I saw that vein pulsing but not this time. This was a fight I had to win. I sensed that my life, my future depended on it.

Steeling my nerves and clenching my fists, I tried to speak calmly while I gave the speech I had rehearsed dozens of times. "I appreciate your wanting to make sure I'm on the right track with my life. I know you want what's best for me, but right now I think you are suggesting what is best for you."

Dad started to argue but I held up my hand in the stop gesture. "Please let me finish. I am attracted to girls. It's my biological make up, and there is nothing I can do about it. I know it seems a sudden, drastic change, and I'm not sure why it took me so long to admit to myself that I am gay. I think it had something to do with being taught that homosexuality is a sin plus not wanting to disappoint you two.

"But once I accepted who I am, there was no turning back. I am homosexual, period. I believe God still loves me, and I hope you will, too." *I got that out without my tongue sticking to the roof of my mouth! Dad's vein is still pulsing. I'd better brace myself for what is coming.*

He sputtered. "How… You… What…"

"Honey let's see how this sounds. Why don't you go through the Sword of Grace program and see if you still feel that way afterwards. If you do, then we will know that is what's right for you. Either way, you will be sure about yourself and who you are," Mom intervened.

I had anticipated that line of reasoning and was prepared. *Maybe I should be on the debate team.* "Mom, first of all I don't need testing by fire to help me be sure of my identity. Secondly, have you read about that program? It is basically a brainwashing program to scare people to change their identities. I can't believe you would even consider putting me through something like that."

Dad's vein pulsed faster. He stopped sputtering and exploded. "How dare you talk to us like that! We are your parents and know what is best for you! You are going to that program, so you might as well accept it and start planning what to pack!"

I'm pretty sure the windows were rattling with the volume of his voice.

"Hon, the neighbors don't need to hear our business," Mom said.

"I don't care if the whole world knows we are trying to be responsible parents!" The volume was toned down a bit, though. "I want Willow to know that she will be going to Sword of Grace the day after Christmas, and that's that!"

He gave me the death stare this time. I looked at Will, hoping for support. I could tell by his eyes he had nothing. If I have a vein in my temple, I'm sure it was pulsing like mad. "I… will… not… go… to… that… place." I slid my chair back and stomped out of the room before the tears could start.

Rage and pain collided in my heart, creating a tsunami of tears. I flopped on the bed, buried my face in the pillow, and sobbed. After a few minutes there was a knock on the door.

"Go away!"

The door opened. "Honey, are you OK?"

"Go away!" I screamed. She shut the door, and I got up and locked it. The pillow case was wet, so I turned it over. The tears started to slow, and I started breathing normally again. Hearing a soft scratch and a hoarse meow, I let Taz in.

She hopped onto the bed with me and rubbed her chin on my cheek. Then she purred and cuddled up next to me. She always knew how to comfort me when I was upset. I lay there and tried to think what I could do to convince them that Sword of Grace was a bad idea.

There is no convincing them. What else can I do? I thought some more. *I don't imagine anyone goes to that program willingly, but I'm not going at all*!

I turned onto my side and ran my fingers through the luscious hair on the back of Taz's neck. She purred louder. *I have to study for my calculus test* kept interrupting my thoughts. Suddenly a plan crystalized. *I know what I have to do.*

Chapter 29

Friday, December 21, 2018

At 3:59am I turned off the alarm on my phone and slid out of bed. Taz was between me and the wall, so I hardly disturbed her. I hadn't slept. I had spent the time planning.

As quietly as I could, I pulled a duffle bag out of the closet. I grabbed the outfits I had worked out in my head, folded them, and packed them in the duffle bag. I was nervous, so my folding lacked the neatness I usually achieved. *It will have to do.* I moved on to the next step.

Tiptoeing to the bathroom, I packed toiletries and two rolls of toilet paper. *It will be cold.* I crept back to my room and removed the blanket from my bed before making it up. Taz was not pleased. I added my sleeping bag to the pile.

Taz rubbed against my leg and meowed. While I scratched her ear like she loved, a wave of sadness made my heart heavy. I wasn't sure I could stand leaving her. She looked at me with her beautiful green eyes as if she could read my thoughts. I saw pleading in her expression.

OK, I'll do it. On the spur of the moment I decided she was going with me. *I'll need food, water, and litter.* She meowed. "Yes, of course. Treats, too," I whispered.

I mentally ran through my inventory of clothes and toiletries to make sure I had everything. Nothing seemed to be missing.

Oops! Phone charger. I added that to the bag. I placed the bag, blanket, and sleeping bag on the bed, then checked to make sure I hadn't forgotten anything else. I started to turn out the light but decided I could say I was up early studying if someone caught me.

On my way to the kitchen, I knocked a chair with the blanket. I froze, fearing someone would get up to check on the noise. *The middle of the night is so silent.* Hearing no feet hit the floor, I continued on.

I started to put down my things then decided to go ahead and put them in the Jeep. There would be less evidence if someone got up. I stopped at the door. This would be the loudest noise I would make, other than hitting the chair. I changed my mind. *I'll wait and just go out the door once.*

I put everything down on the floor and went to gather food, litter and treats. *I need something to serve as a litter box. Hmmm.* Then I remembered there was a box the perfect size waiting to be recycled. I lined it with two trash bags and added litter. I checked my watch: 4:27. *Not too bad. Now to get all of this to the car without getting caught.*

I took a deep breath, unlocked the deadbolt, and opened the door as quietly as I could. *That wasn't bad.* I loaded my arms, pushed open the storm door with my elbow, and slid out. *Ooh! Cold! Should have worn a jacket!* I worked open the door and stuffed bag, blanket, and sleeping bag into the back seat.

Leaving the car door open, I retrieved the litter box, two plastic bowls, and two bottles of water. *I hope the water doesn't freeze. I hope Taz doesn't freeze.* I had originally thought I would go ahead and leave her in the car. *I need a new plan. Ah! I'll bring her out just before everyone gets up.*

Taz was meowing when I came back in. "Shhhh." I saw she was eyeing the treat bag, so I slipped her a few and put the bag up. I slinked back to my room and checked the time: 4:52. In less than an hour I had packed my escape. *There is no way I'm going to that terrifying place.*

My nerves were zinging. *No point in going back to bed.* I decided to try looking at calculus a little more. When I sat down, it hit me. *I need to leave Will a note. He is my rock.*

I aimed the pen at the paper, but it refused to write. *What do I say to him? God, help me to write this.* After breathing the prayer, words came.

Dear Will,

I love you so much. By the time you find this, I will have disappeared. I am running away to keep from going to Sword of Grace. I will probably be back after Christmas break. We'll see. Please don't try to find me. My phone will be off so that I can't be tracked. I hope you have a merry Christmas.

Love, Willow.

P.S. I have Taz with me. I just couldn't leave her.

I whipped my hand to my cheek to keep a tear from dripping onto the paper. I would miss Will. I would miss Christmas. But I just couldn't bear the alternative. *I wish my parents could be reasonable and just accept me.*

More tears flowed. *No! I have to stop this! I am doing what I have to do to take care of myself. I shall have no regrets.*

I folded the paper and put it in the outside pocket of my backpack. *I'll leave it on his windshield when I leave school.*

I looked at a calculus problem. My eyes were on the page, but my mind was on running away. Then I realized I was seeing two of everything. I suddenly felt so tired. *I am so going to fail this test! I need lots of coffee this morning.*

I checked my watch: 5:23. *Twenty-two minutes till Dad's alarm goes off. What if he gets up early? At five thirty, I'll put Taz in the Jeep. I'll leave for school early to study before the test.* The school opens at 7:10 for students to arrive. I could leave at 6:55. *Taz will be OK. She does have a fur coat.*

At 5:30, I scooped Taz up, loaded her into the car, and whispered. "I'll be back in a little while." She looked at me like I had lost my mind. Maybe she was right.

Slipping back into the house, I turned on the kitchen light and made coffee. I went back to my room and made sure my calculus book was open on the desk so it would look like I had been studying.

Sadness crept in as I arranged the book. I looked around at the familiar surroundings. *I'll miss this place. Oh, I almost forgot my diary!* I pulled it out of the nightstand and worked it into my backpack.

Dad's feet hit the floor. In less than five minutes, he would come out to do his exercise routine. I was glad he worked at staying fit, even though he wasn't my favorite person at the moment.

I hurried to the desk and sat down. Pencil poised on the paper, I tried to work out the steps and timing of my escape. Nervousness pushed the sadness aside. I took a deep breath and let it out slowly. Then I told myself, "I have this all worked out. There is nothing to be nervous about."

A soft knock. "Come in."

"What are you doing up so early?" Dad asked.

"I have a calculus test today."

"Good luck," and he closed the door.

I watched the time. At six o'clock I got dressed, then went and ate breakfast. I poured coffee into a thermos and left it open to cool for a few minutes. *I hate the feel of a scalded tongue.*

Mom appeared in the kitchen in her robe. She asked the same question, "What are you doing up so early?"

I gave the same answer. "I have a calculus test today." So far I had told no lies. Chalk one up for me, but it was time to change that.

"I already gave Taz her treats. She was begging." I hoped that would explain her not being in the kitchen looking for her tasty morsels. Now that I think of it, that was technically not a lie either. I had given Taz her treats. I don't know why that made me feel better, but it did. I didn't like to lie to my parents.

Back in my room, I checked my watch: 6:37. *Eighteen minutes till time to leave.* I heard Will come out of his room and head to the bathroom. Leaving him would be the hardest. *What will I do without my twin beside me?* I wondered if I could risk sending a text when I figured out where I would be. *Maybe he could visit.*

Time crept. I was too nervous to get sleepy, so I just waited. Finally it was 6:43. *That's close enough.* I packed the calculus book and went to the kitchen. Mom was eating.

"I'm going on to school so I can study right up to the bell." Another true statement.

"It's still a little early. You'll get there before the doors open.

"I need to get gas. I'm nearly on empty." OK, that was a half-truth. I did want to get gas, but I had over a quarter of a tank. I pulled the door open before any probing questions could follow.

"Good luck on the test," Mom said as I walked out.

"Thanks," I called back.

I peered into the Jeep. I had to make sure Taz didn't escape when I opened the door. She was curled up on the blanket in the back seat. I jumped in.

"You forgot your coffee," Mom called from the door.

Great. Taz stood and stretched. I hopped out and got the coffee from Mom. "Thanks! You saved me."

Chapter 30

Friday, December 21, 2018

I was glad to hear the door close as I walked back to the Jeep. Taz was still on the blanket. "OK. I'm off. I hope I'm doing the right thing, Lord."

After filling up with gas, I stopped by the ATM and withdrew two hundred dollars. "I hope that will be enough," I said to Taz. I knew the police could track my debit card if I used it, at least I had seen that on TV.

I parked and took the coffee and backpack. "You just relax, and I'll be back in about an hour," I told Taz. "The sun should warm things up in here. I'm on my way to fail a calculus test."

I really hoped I wouldn't fail, but I felt so unprepared as I walked toward the school. I was also distracted by thoughts of running away. *What will I do? Where will I go? I will just have to trust you to lead me, Lord. That's the only thing I know to do. Will you be with me?*

That thought still plagued me. *Does God still love me? I hope so. I feel like you do. I feel like you created me, and you love the being you created. So that should include me, right?*

I was hoping for a definite answer, maybe a light, a rainbow, something to let me know for certain. "I guess certainty is not really your thing, is it, Lord?" I said aloud as I neared the school. "Please help me with this test. We'll take it one step at a time today. Thanks." With that last prayer I opened the door and walked into the hallway.

I turned the corner and was surprised to see other students in the hallway. *I guess we are doing the same thing.* It surprised me how long it took to comprehend what I was seeing: three guys with hoodies were walking toward my locker. My heart gave a giant beat and then began to race. I almost shouted at them before realizing they didn't know I was there.

I walked faster to try to catch up while I pulled my phone from my pocket. I started videotaping. Holding the phone up to capture their image, I closed the gap between us.

What are you doing? my rational self protested. My angry self drove me on. As I hurried, my purse shifted and slung forward. Apparently one of them heard. When turned to look, the ski mask seemed like something out of a horror film. I froze in place.

"Hey, look! It's the lesbo!" All three looked at me, the face masks sending a chill down my spine. *That might have been Wyatt's voice.* The one who heard me first started toward me. My heart pounded in my ears. I braced myself for a fight and scrambled in my purse for the mace. *Where is it?*

He got closer as I frantically dug, feeling for the cylindrical can of salvation. I didn't dare look down.

"Come back. She's videotaping us," one of the guys called. As he turned back toward the group, I finally found the canister.

"Here's our love note for today," the one who had called the other back said.

He's the leader. I watched as they taped a note on my locker. I kept the phone aimed at them while I pulled the mace out of my purse. *I need to be ready.* I risked looking down long enough to make sure it was aimed correctly.

I heard whispering but couldn't make out what they were saying. *I have to wait till they are close enough before shooting the mace.* My palms were sweaty. The whispering was unnerving. I walked toward them.

Without a word, they turned their backs and walked away. I stood where I was until they turned the corner. I walked to the locker and videotaped the note. At the bottom it said, "Flames Reserved For You."

Another chill flowed through my spine. *Are they planning to burn me like a witch? OK, that was a horrible thought. I have to stop the negativity in my brain.* I stood staring at the note. Each one was getting uglier.

Another jolt hit my nervous system. *I don't have time to deal with the police today.* I snatched the paper off my locker, wadded it up, and stuffed it into my purse. Footsteps sounded from behind. It was Mr. Carlisle.

As I opened my locker, he said, "Good morning, early bird."

"Good morning. I need all the study time I can get. Do you mind if I come on into the room?"

"That's fine. I'm sure you will do well on the test. You always do."

"Thanks." I wished I felt that confident. But with all the distractions and stress, I felt the exact opposite. I went to my desk and tried to focus.

Myra and Liia came into the room together. "Well, look who's already here," Myra said. "I thought I'd be the earliest."

"Hey!" I said. I had to hide my stress to keep from revealing my plan to them. No one could know. *No, I can't tell them. I have to resist the urge. I can't risk their trying to stop me. I will not end up at Sword of Grace.*

"You look stressed," Liia said, touching my shoulder.

"I am. I'm afraid I'm not going to do well on this test." Her hand seemed to send comfort through my shoulder to my heart.

"From what I've seen, you're great at math. You will outscore the rest of us," Liia encouraged.

"Thanks for the positive vibes," I said. "I think I'm going to need them."

"We have fifteen minutes for a last-minute review," Myra said. "I'm going to get cracking!"

Myra and Liia sat down. My mind raced ahead. *Liia will walk with me to second period. How will I get away from her? The note! I'll tell her I have to go to the office about it. In fact, I can tell Liia and Myra.*

With my escape plan set, my nerves seemed to settle. *OK, Lord, it's time for a calculus test. Please help me to do my best and help me remember what I have learned. I need you. Amen.*

Mr. Carlisle handed out the tests. The first problem was easy. *That was nice of him. It helps build confidence.* I moved to the second one. It was a little harder, but I felt sure I got it right. I finished the last problem with a smile. *Could I have made a hundred?*

Doubt slipped back in, and I decided I should check my work. There were a few problems I was unsure about as I looked back over them. *I'll trust my first answers.*

"Please hand in your tests," Mr. Carlisle announced. A couple of minutes later, the bell rang. I gathered my backpack and purse and walked out with Myra and Liia.

"That wasn't bad for a calculus test," Myra said.

"I agree," Liia responded.

"I hate to jinx myself, but I thought I did well, too." My nerves began to tense. I thought about when to say I had to go to the office while Myra and Liia chatted. *I'll wait till we get near the room and pretend I forgot.*

"Christmas break begins tomorrow!" I said, trying to sound happy.

"I can't wait to see my grandparents," Liia said. "But I'll miss seeing you two."

"We'll miss you, but maybe we can Facetime," I offered.

"That would be great! Sweden is six hours ahead of the time here, so we will have to take that into account."

Myra peeled off to go to her class. Liia and I were almost to the classroom when I said, "I forgot that I found another note on my locker this morning." I pulled showed Liia.

"That's terrible," she said.

"I have to turn this in at the office. I didn't want to deal with it before the calculus test."

"I wish they would stop harassing you. I'll see you when you get back."

I walked toward the office, feeling sad that Liia would be gone for two weeks. The sadness moved toward stress as I realized what I was about to do. *I'll be gone for two weeks, too! God, please walk me through this. I have no idea what I am doing.* With that I walked out of the building and into the unknown.

Chapter 31

Friday, December 21, 2018

Checking to make sure Taz wouldn't jump out, I slid into the Jeep. "Did you miss me?" I asked the cat. She looked up from her spot on the blanket and meowed. It sounded more like, "I want to go home," than, "I missed you."

A twinge of guilt stung as I cranked the Jeep. Maybe I should have left her at the house, but I needed her with me. Sadness washed in as I powered down my phone.

Backing out of the parking space, a new problem dawned on me. Officer Benefield would be at the exit and would want to see a check out note.

"Hmmm. I need an idea, and I need it now!" I was nearing the gate and nearing panic mode when the answer came. Officer Benefield stepped out of the booth as anticipated. I pulled up and rolled down my window.

"Hey, Willow. I need to see your check out slip."

I "checked" my pockets to find it wasn't there. "I must have left it in the bathroom."

"Why are you leaving?"

"It's embarrassing. My period started, and I don't have any supplies."

"OK, just let me check with the office." He pulled out his phone and stepped into the booth. I guess he was going to call to verify that I had checked out. I seized the opportunity to take off. Another twinge of guilt pinged.

I wonder what he will do. Would he put out an alert to have the police track me down? That thought helped my plan to crystalize. *I can't stay in Hawksville. I've always liked Chattanooga. I think I'll go there.*

I tried to obey the speed limit and kept looking in the mirror for flashing blue lights. I took Highway 111 and headed south. When I left the city limits of Hawksville, I tried to relax my white-knuckled grip on the steering wheel.

"OK, we have about forty-five minutes to plan, Taz. We're going to need food, more litter, water… anything else?"

"Meow."

"Of course! Treats. I was startled when Taz jumped into my lap. She curled up and purred. Soon she was asleep.

I had been to Chattanooga many times but had never paid attention to things like grocery stores and certainly not to places to hide. The further I drove, the more nervous I became. I was white knuckling the steering wheel again. "I can't believe I am doing this."

A sign pointing to Shady Grove appeared. *That sounds like a nice place.* I pulled off and found myself driving south along the river. A grocery store came into view up ahead. "Thanks, Lord. This must be the spot."

Taz was still asleep in my lap. I made a quick list and thought through it twice to make sure I had everything we would need.

"OK Taz, I have to get out." She stood and stretched. I scooped her up and put her on the blanket. "I'll be back in a jiffy."

Supplied with granola bars, trail mix, apples, bananas, cat food, litter, treats, and water, I headed south again. I passed an old factory on the left. It wasn't till about a half a mile down the road that it dawned on me that no cars were in the parking lot.

I turned around to check it out. *This place looks dilapidated.* I didn't see signs of anyone around. Tentatively, I pulled around behind the building. There were woods behind the factory. I assumed they went all the way to the river.

"Taz, I think we've found our new home. What do you think?" She hopped back into my lap. "As long as you have loving, a soft place to sleep, and food, you're happy. I guess my life will be that simple, too, at least for a while."

Turning off the Jeep turned on the silence. I checked my watch: 10:43. The sun warmed the Jeep. I leaned back and gave Taz a long scratch on the ear.

An awful smell woke me up. I sat up straight, trying to figure out where I was. My brain finally got into gear, and I remembered the events of the morning. I also discerned the source of the smell.

"Really, Taz? I was sleeping so good." I stretched and realized I had to do something about the litter. The scoop was in the second bag I searched. When I opened the back door, I told Taz to stay put. She didn't seem inclined to jump out. Holding the poop in the scoop, I decided to dump it in the woods.

I took a diagonal path from the car. "This will be the cat toileting area." I made that mental note so I wouldn't step in it when it was my turn. I passed a fire ring and wished I had supplies for s'mores. I started to walk into the woods, then decided just to toss it. A chilling wind blew, and I hurried back to the car.

After jumping into the driver's seat, I eyed the passenger seat. "That would probably be more comfortable for just lounging." I scooted over. With the smell improved, my tummy rumbled. It was 1:13. "Wow, Taz. I slept for two hours."

Taz hopped into my lap and rubbed her chin to mine. "Thanks. I love you, too. I think it's time to eat. Do you want a treat?"

"Meow."

I hadn't planned out placement of food and water for Taz. Looking around, I decided the best place would be the floorboard in the back seat on the opposite side from the litter. I had to get out to find her bowls and set up the food and water. I fished out a granola bar, apple, and water for myself and hopped back into the passenger seat.

Rubbing my hands on my legs, I said, "It's cold outside." I pulled out my phone to check the weather before I remembered I had turned it off. Looking at the blank screen, I suddenly felt alone. Anxiety fluttered in my heart.

No. I won't feel that way. I can do this. I have to do this. Otherwise I'll end up stuck at Sword of Grace. I just have to keep reminding myself of the alternative.

Taz jumped back into my lap. I knew she could sense my despair. She snuggled up and purred. "I'm glad I have you," I told her.

Time moved like a slug as the sun crossed the sky. With Taz curled up for yet another nap, my mind wandered. *What would Myra and Liia be doing now? It's four o'clock, so Liia is probably packing to leave for Sweden. Myra is probably curled up with a book in front of the fireplace. What did they think when I disappeared from school? I hope they aren't out looking for me. I'm sure Will told them what's going on.*

A couple of minutes later my thoughts switched gears. *I wonder if this is what homeless people do. How do they keep from getting bored out of their minds? I guess they don't have to keep their phones turned off to keep parents from tracking them. Of course, they may not be able to afford a phone.*

Finally it was 5:00. The sun had dipped behind the trees and cold oozed in with the shadows. "Taz, we have to get ready for nighttime," I announced, realizing it would be nearly dark by 5:30. I thought through what needed to be done. *Scoop the litter, get out what I'm eating for supper, figure out how to sleep.* I don't know why this hadn't dawned on me before, but I would have to use the bathroom.

OK. Let's think this through. I'll need toilet paper and a place. I looked back. *I guess the place is the woods.* I cringed at the thought. *I'll do everything else first.* Getting out of the Jeep, I gasped at the cutting wind. "It's going to be freezing tonight," I explained to Taz.

I busied myself with preparations. I emptied the back seat, moved Taz's food and water to the floor of the passenger seat, put her bed where the food and water had been, and spread out the sleeping bag and blanket on the back seat. I lined up the food bags so I could reach them just behind the back seat.

The sun was threatening to leave me in the dark when I had finished. I took a deep breath, pulled out the toilet paper, and eyed the woods. This seemed odd, but I suddenly feared stepping into the place I had gone previously the next time I had to use the bathroom. I decided to count my steps and use a different formula each time.

Pausing at the edge of the asphalt, I created the plan. *I'll go one hundred steps ahead, then fifty to the right.* I made my way in, counting each step. At one hundred, I turned ninety degrees to the right and marked off fifty steps. I was right next to a tree and could hear the water from the river. *Perfect.*

I hurried back and hopped into the Jeep. "Goodness, Taz! It's cold!" The warmth we had had earlier was leaving. At least the wind was kept at bay.

Darkness descended far more quickly than I would have liked. I used a flashlight to organize supper: trail mix and grapes. *I wonder if the water will be frozen in the morning.* I stuck two bottles into the sleeping bag just in case.

I got colder and colder as I sat there. It was 6:15. I crawled into the sleeping bag, arranged the blanket over me, and pulled Taz inside. "This is going to be a long night."

Chapter 32

Saturday, December 22, 2018

I awoke to darkness. It was warm and snuggly in the sleeping bag, but my nose was cold. I could feel Taz next to my head. Working my arm up, cold rushed in as I checked my watch. It was 4:42, way too early to get up. I scrunched down farther into the sleeping bag and closed my eyes.

The next time I awoke, dim light floated on the darkness. My soul was uneasy, like something was after me. A dream wormed back into my consciousness. I let it play out in my mind and discovered it was the source of my distress.

I was in dark woods. A thin moon provided just enough light to see the trunks of trees. There was total silence till a twig broke. Another broken twig signaled footsteps. Someone or something was in the woods and coming closer.

"Who's there?" I called, then slapped my hand to my mouth. I had just given away my location. The steps quickened. It was after me. I tried to run but kept hitting branches. My jacket snagged on something and wouldn't let go. The sound of breaking twigs was getting closer. Roger's face seemed to float in the sky where the moon should have been. That's when I woke up.

"I'm surprised I slept so good. I guess being up all night last night could have had something to do with it," I confided to

Taz. She stood, stretched, and crawled a little farther into the sleeping bag.

"Thank you, Lord, for letting me sleep." I had expected to lie awake feeling afraid someone would discover my Jeep parked in this desolate spot. I twisted onto my side, careful not to knock Taz off the narrow seat.

I was still anxious about the dream. Roger's face kept coming back into focus. *I wonder what that dream means. Roger had an accusing look on his face. Lord, is that you or Roger telling me I am wrong. Can it really be a sin to be who you created me to be? That doesn't seem fair. Maybe you didn't create me this way. Maybe I am just making all of this up. I wish I could know for sure.*

My mind spun, running in circles over and over those thoughts. It was exhausting. *I have to stop and think of something else! On a normal Saturday, I would sleep till at least nine. It's only seven fourteen.* I scratched Taz's ear for a minute and then tried to go back to sleep. I couldn't get comfortable. Then it dawned on me. *I have to pee.*

I put my hand out of the sleeping bag. *I can hold it!* My bladder cramped and said, "No you can't!"

"Sorry, Taz. I have to get up." She had learned the phrase "get up" because I always said before standing. She didn't move.

"I know it's cold, but I have to go." I gently set her on the floor and worked myself out of the sleeping bag. I slid on my shoes and just stuffed the laces down inside. "Wow! It's cold."

I took a moment to recall last night's formula for my toilet location. *OK, I'll go one hundred steps in and fifty to the left today.* I hurried to the woods and started counting steps. While pulling my pants back up I heard movement nearby, and the dream rushed back into my mind.

I was already freezing, so it's hard to say I froze. The sound got closer. A bunny hopped by. I felt silly for being so scared and hurried back to the car.

A thin film of ice had covered part of the surface of Taz's water. I wiggled back into the sleeping bag and patted the seat beside me. Taz climbed back in.

After having slept for twelve hours, I knew I wouldn't go back to sleep. So I lay there and pondered. "What could we do today, Taz?" I asked. She just put her head back down. I tried to generate some possibilities, but everything I thought of doing involved being outside of the car. I couldn't let Taz loose. I couldn't bear losing her.

"I know! We need a harness!" Pictures of walking through a park with Taz meandered through my mind. "That will at least give us a break from being in the car."

I still had a hundred and forty dollars after my grocery run. I started to reach for my phone to locate a pet store and remembered I couldn't turn it on. *There has to be another way. What would people have done before cell phones?*

My tummy rumbled, and I temporarily lost the scent of that trail. Sitting up, I saw that Taz still had enough food in her bowl. I pulled another granola bar, apple, and water from the bag and had my breakfast, still wrapped in the sleeping bag.

While munching on the apple a solution dawned on me. "I could stop and ask where a pet store is." *I'm talking to myself!* Having a plan lightened my heart. The day no longer seemed so empty. I saved a little of my apple and decided to toss it into the woods. "Maybe the bunny will find it." I set it on the granola bar wrapper to deal with later.

Taz looked cold, so I wrapped her in the blanket with her little head sticking out. She seemed to like that. "I'm glad I brought my book," I said and fished it out of the backpack.

A few pages in, I discovered my mind had drifted to Myra and Liia. *Liia is probably on her way to the airport. They might pass near me. Myra is probably organizing a search party. I wish I could have told her not to worry. Will is probably mad and thinks I did something stupid. I hope my parents are worried.*

That last thought was vindictive. *But they are the reason I'm out here.* I checked my watch: 8:49. "I wonder what time pet stores open?" I asked Taz.

My heart suddenly shifted. The hope going to the pet store brought flipped into a heavy sadness. *I don't know who I am anymore. What does it mean for me to be gay? Will I ever be loved again? I hate to miss Christmas.* Tears began to ooze down my cold cheeks. Taz crawled into my lap and nuzzled me. I hugged her and cried in earnest.

Finally I fished out the toilet paper to clean up my teary mess. "We can't sink into the sadness, Taz. Let's go get you a harness and go for a walk."

Out of the sleeping bag and into the driver's seat, I cranked the Jeep. "I hope you don't mind the heat on high," I warned Taz. I turned left out of the factory lot and drove toward Chattanooga. The Jeep was still cold when I passed the first convenience store, so I kept going.

After a few miles, I couldn't believe my luck. I passed a shopping area with a PetSmart. The cat harness was only $9.99, so I picked a toy, too.

I gasped when I saw a police car pulling through the parking lot. That was the first time I had thought about the probability that they would be looking for my vehicle.

I realized I had frozen right in the doorway when another customer said, "Excuse me, please." I stepped to the side and tried to squelch the rising panic. I hoped what I was feeling inside wasn't showing on my face.

"Sorry, I was just trying to make sure I hadn't forgotten something," I said as she walked on. I was hoping she wouldn't think I was afraid of the police. Apparently my comment didn't even register because the woman just kept walking.

That was good, but I was still standing at the door of the store. My heart urged me to run to the car. My mind told me to walk casually so I wouldn't draw attention to myself. That's what I did, but I walked quickly. I hopped into my Jeep and watched as the patrol car moved along the parking lot in the lane farthest from the store.

When it turned down the lane in which I was parked, I started sweating. I cranked the car. *Should I pull out or stay put?* My heart was racing. My indecision cost me as indecision often does. It was too late to drive toward the patrol car so the officer couldn't see my tag.

I stopped breathing as though that would help hide me. The patrol car passed me and parked three spaces beyond. There were no flashing lights, so I just waited and tried to relax my death grip on the steering wheel.

Do I go now? Do I drive toward the patrol car so my tag is hidden when I back out? The questions paralyzed me, and I just sat and watched like a deer in headlights. *If the officer had recognized my vehicle, I wouldn't still be sitting here.* That thought spurred me to action.

Backing out, I drove away from the threat, hoping the officer wouldn't notice my tag. I could see the officer getting out of the car as I drove away. She appeared not to be paying any attention to me.

I took a deep breath and blew it out hard, hoping to blow some of the panic out with it. "Taz, we have to be more careful. The police might be looking for me." Taz hopped into my lap and curled up.

"I'd like to be a cat. You don't seem to worry about anything."

"Meow."

Chapter 33

Saturday, December 22, 2018

y hands were still shaking as I pulled back behind the abandoned factory. *What if I had been caught? Would they put me in juvenile for running away or just take me back home? If they took me back home, my parents would stick me in a place that's probably worse than juvenile. I have to be more careful. I can't get caught!*

My thoughts continued down that dark road through lunch, which was trail mix. *What is going to become of my life? Will my parents kick me out, and I'll end up living like this? No, that's not happening. I'm finishing high school and going to college, hopefully on a tennis scholarship. I can do that even if I'm living out of my car. Maybe?*

It was a beautiful day and the sun warmed the car nicely. "OK, Taz, let's go for a walk." I opened the harness, and it took three tries to get it on her the right way. She looked insulted.

Setting her on the ground, I said, "Let's see if we can make it to the river." Taz headed under the car. I put a couple of treats down, and she came out. I put a couple more about six feet ahead, and she gobbled those up. Finally she got the idea and walked along with me.

We had to work our way around some briars and thick undergrowth a few times, but finally made it to the water. It was a large creek rather than the river. "I guess this meets up with the river somewhere," I explained to Taz. She didn't look impressed.

There was a nice rock right next to the creek, and I sat down in the sun. Taz sniffed around the various trees and bushes. The water mesmerized me as it moved along. There were rocks a few feet downstream that created chutes, making a soothing sound.

It was so peaceful sitting there. The water seemed to take away the stress as it flowed on by. I sat and watched, enjoying the little swirls and eddies. This was the calmest I had felt in a long time. "Thank you, Lord, for this wonderful place."

I didn't notice it at first, but it finally dawned on me what I was seeing. A feather floated slowly by, spinning for a moment in the pool. It had an orangey-red color on the tip. I wanted to catch it, but it was too far to reach. I watched and wondered. *What's a feather doing in the water? Birds are supposed to be in the air.* I chuckled at the thought and watched it flow on downstream.

I jumped when I realized I had forgotten about Taz. She was lying down and appeared to be enjoying the scenery. "This is a nice place, isn't it?" She looked at me and looked back at the river without comment.

My backside began to hurt, so I stood and stretched. A shiver went up my spine, and I realized I was getting cold. "Taz, I think it's time to go back to the car."

Taz didn't seem to mind the chill. "You're wearing a fur coat, so it doesn't bother you," I explained. We made our way back to the Jeep. I was surprised at how quickly Taz had taken to the harness. She was a natural, and I wished I had taken her for walks a long time ago. "Oh, well, it's best not to dwell on the past."

"OK. It's two thirty-four. Now what?" I leaned the passenger seat back and closed my eyes. Taz curled up in my lap, and I scratched the back of her neck. I was always amazed at how wonderfully soft her fur was in that spot.

I started counting the days on my fingers. "Fourteen or fifteen more days to live in my car, depending on whether I go back Saturday or Sunday. I might get away with going back Friday evening. Ugh! So far we've made it a little over twenty-four hours. This is going to be a long two weeks."

Next I found myself praying. *Lord, my life is such a mess right now. I'm sorry that I'm screwing everything up. I hope you will forgive me and still love me. I never dreamed the discovery that I'm homosexual would lead to such problems.*

You seem to still be with me. Why can't my parents accept me? Why can't Roger accept me? I believe you when you said you so loved the world that you gave your only son so that whoever believes in you shouldn't perish but have everlasting life.

I believe in you. Don't I count? Tears were warming my cheeks.

I'm trying to love people like you told me to. It's not like I just decided one day to be attracted to girls. I tried to like boys, but it just doesn't work. I think you made me this way, and you said you looked over all that you had made and said it was good. I hope that includes me, too.

I suddenly felt as if God was right there in the car with me. In fact, I looked around to see if I could see anyone. It was still just Taz and me. The feeling didn't go away.

I closed my eyes and went back to praying. *Lord, thank you for being here with me.*

It was more like I felt the words rather than hearing them, but they seemed real. "You are very much loved, my child, and I have plans for you. I want you to minister in my church, to love people into my kingdom, and to spread grace in this world."

I think I stopped breathing. As my heart processed what it had heard, the tears flowed faster. Warmth flowed through my veins, and I felt wrapped in deep love. I don't know how long I sat there before realizing what God was asking- no calling- me to do.

But Lord, the church won't even let me speak at Youth Sunday. How could I possibly go into the ministry?

Another clear heart-heard voice came to me. "I will open the doors if you will follow."

My hands were cold, but somehow my palms were sweating. I sensed this Presence was waiting for an answer. I couldn't see how this could possibly happen. I also couldn't say no. With muscles tensing and heart pounding, I said, "Yes, Lord. I will follow wherever you lead me."

A strange feeling flooded my heart. I guess the best way to describe it is happiness- no joy. I felt truly joyful. I felt with certainty that it didn't matter what people thought of me. God was with me and loved me.

After the wonderful joy, a nervous excitement set in. My whole future had shifted. *What does it take to become a minister? I think they go to school for that. Can I still go to college on a tennis scholarship? This is going to take some research!*

"I need to write this moment down!" I scrambled to get out my diary to record what had just happened. The joy lasted while I hurriedly wrote down my experience.

I sat back smiling. I felt affirmed and loved, at least till a wave of doubt rolled in. *The church won't let me become a minister. How is that going to happen?*

I nearly jumped when I heard in my heart, "Have faith, my child."

"OK," I said. "I will just have to trust you on that one and be obedient to your call."

I felt like I should pray or something. Then it dawned on me that the whole experience had been a prayer. "Thank you, Lord," I whispered.

I looked out at the ugly back of the factory. *Why don't I change my perspective?* I turned the Jeep around to face the woods. *Much better. Instead of looking at decay, I'm looking at life!*

The sun had sunk below the tops of the trees just enough to cast a shadow over the Jeep. The toasty warmth began to fade. I checked my watch, and it was already 4:22.

"It will be dark and cold soon," I announced to Taz. I looked around for her but didn't see her. The scratch of litter and sudden aroma announced her location.

"It's time for some housekeeping." I got out, scooped the litter, and followed the diagonal path to the cat toilet. I replenished her food and water then decided I would take a turn at toileting before it got dark.

This time it's one hundred steps in and twenty-five to the right.

The wind chilled my bones. When I hopped back into the Jeep, I said, "I think it's going to be even colder tonight. We'll have to do some serious snuggling."

"Meow," Taz said from where she was eating.

The trees were tall, but I could still see some pink and orange as the sun set. The temperature seemed to drop as quickly as the light faded. "I had better eat and get into the sleeping bag."

I was trying to summon the gumption to eat another granola bar when I remembered the Taco Bell I had seen on the way to PetSmart. The call of a hot taco won.

"It's dark, so I will be less likely to be noticed by the police. I can use the drive through," I rationalized. "OK, Taz. Let's go for a ride."

When I hopped out of the back seat, I heard the loud throb of bass music. It slowed as it passed in front of the factory. I knew a vehicle was turning in. *This can't be good!*

Chapter 34

Saturday, December 22, 2018

I jumped into the front seat as quickly as I could, and my hands shook as I fumbled to get the keys out of my purse. The music blared as three vehicles rounded the corner of the factory, lights shining right at me.

I missed the ignition twice trying to insert the key. "I have to get out of here!" Two pickups and an SUV parked around me as I cranked my Jeep to life. There was just enough room for me to squeeze through. I gunned the accelerator and flew through the gap. The SUV tried to maneuver to cut me off, but I was going too fast.

I zoomed out of the parking lot, hitting some serious bumps, and turned left. I still wanted that taco. "Really?" I was shocked to see them come out to follow me.

I was afraid to risk exceeding the speed limit and getting pulled over, so they easily caught up with me. One tried to pass me, but a car came from the other direction.

"What am I going to do?" I checked my mirrors almost as much as I looked ahead. "Lord, help me! OK, try to think. I need to get to an area where there are people. PetSmart. That's the only place I know."

They tried to pass again. No cars were coming from the other direction. *If they get in front of me, they can force me to stop!*

I floored the accelerator and cut the other vehicle off as we came to a curve. We were finally coming into a populated area. That seemed good till the traffic light turned red. I didn't dare stop. I didn't dare run it. "Now what to do?"

I slowed down at the light, then turned right, achieving a honk from the car I had pulled in front of. My pursuers followed suit.

"I have to find my way to PetSmart." I took the next two lefts and came back to the road that I knew led to the store. They were still behind me.

I could see the parking lot ahead on the right and began to think I would make it. Without using my turn signal, I whipped into the parking lot and drove toward PetSmart. They pulled in behind me, and I tightened my grip on the steering wheel even more.

I'm not sure I breathed until they turned left down a lane and headed out of the parking lot. I backed into a parking place as close to the store as I could get and watched, ready to run into the store.

"That was way too scary, Taz!" I sat there and willed my heart to slow down. Finally I let go of the steering wheel and stretched my stiff fingers.

I'm not sure how long I sat there. I didn't look at my watch. I did keep my eyes on the entrance to the parking lot. "I have never been that scared in my life!" I confided to Taz.

My stomach rumbled. "We have to come up with a new place to hide, but I can't think straight on an empty stomach." I decided to take a chance on getting to Taco Bell.

After picking up my order in the drive through, I circled around and backed into a parking space. I checked my watch, and it was 7:16. A steady stream of people came and went, making me feel safer.

After finishing my two Taco Supremes, I still had no idea what to do. "We can't sit here all night because it will close," I explained to Taz, who seemed disappointed I didn't share the tacos. I gave her some treats, which made her happier.

"We can't go back to the factory. I can only imagine what they are doing back there. I wonder what they would have done had they caught us." I couldn't bear to dwell on that, so I went back to the problem at hand.

What are we going to do? I can't risk driving the streets all night. I'm bound to run across a cop. It's too dark to find another place.

I was breathing short and fast. "I have to calm down." I made myself breathe in deep and blow out slowly. It took ten breaths before I felt calmer. As I released the last breath, an idea entered my mind. *An apartment complex! I could find an empty parking space and pull in there. Since it's dark, maybe no one will notice.*

I thought through the steps I needed to take. I scooped Taz's litter and put it in my food bag. I dropped that into the trashcan as I went in to use the bathroom. When I came back, I announced, "Surely there's an apartment complex around here somewhere."

The road we were on seemed promising, so I drove past PetSmart. About half a mile down the road, there it was. I pulled in and circled what seemed a nice complex. There were a few empty spaces across from one of the buildings, so I backed into one.

Climbing into the back seat, I wiggled into the sleeping bag. The heat generated by the heater left in a hurry. "Come on, Taz," I encouraged and patted the seat next to my head. She crawled into the bag with me.

I lay there recounting the events of the day, especially my encounter with God. It made me smile. At some point in the night I fell asleep.

Sunday, December 23, 2018

Pounding on the window startled me awake. I looked up through the frosty window and saw an angry face. "Get out of here or I'll call the police! We don't allow homeless people to live here!" He pounded the window again.

I sat up in my sleeping bag, and he took a step back. *He's afraid of me,* registered in my mind. "OK, I'm going." I yelled loudly enough to get through the window. He waited.

As I worked my way out of the sleeping bag, the cold slapped me. Taz was crouched in the back corner of the Jeep as far away from this crazy man as she could get. I got out on the passenger side because he was standing on the driver's side. He quickly got into his car, which was parked next to mine.

I must be quite the sight! I hadn't showered since Friday morning. My bladder protested as I rounded the Jeep. *I have to find a place to pee in a hurry!* The man glared at me as I got into my car, and I couldn't help glaring back, feeling angry more at the fact that he had scared Taz than that he was running me off.

I drove out of the apartment complex with one thing on my mind: bathroom. That thought was soon joined with another: coffee. *If I go in to buy coffee, I can use the restroom. I wonder if this is how homeless folks get by.*

Miraculously, a Burger King appeared. "A Caramel Frappe! And a toilet!" I backed into a parking place and said, "I'm getting good at this." The Jeep was right between the lines.

I hopped into the back seat, placed my coffee into the cup holder, and fished out a granola bar. "I'm sorry that mean old man scared you," I said, petting Taz. "Maybe this will help." I put some treats on the seat.

I ate the granola bar, pulled out my diary, and wrote about last night's events while I sipped my coffee. It was still cold in the car, so I leaned up into the front seat and cranked the Jeep. "We'll let it run long enough to warm us up," I explained to Taz.

"Meow."

Sometimes it seemed she really understood what I was saying. The Jeep warmed up, and the Caramel Frappe was wonderful. The last sip of coffee brought a dark thought. Well, technically two dark thoughts.

First, *I sure could use a bath!* I had splashed water on my face in the restroom, but that just didn't suffice.

Second, *What are we going to do now?* The abandoned factory had been the perfect place to set up house. "I could assume the guys who ran me off last night were just there to party, and I could reclaim the place now. But what if they came back, and I couldn't get away? No, I can't go back there. I guess we'll have to hunt a new home, Taz."

I cut the Jeep off to save gas. Plus, I felt guilty polluting the air just to be warm. A police car pulled into the parking lot. I cringed and dove down onto the back seat. My heart was pounding in my ears as I waited.

When I could stand it no longer, I lifted my head to peek out. The patrol car was in the drive through line. I took a deep breath and calmed myself.

"Maybe this isn't the best place to stay, Taz."

Chapter 35

Sadness seeped into my soul as I waited for the police car to be gone. *Tomorrow is Christmas Eve. I'm going to miss the candlelight service. I'm going to miss opening presents. I'm going to miss everything!*

For some reason, Grace popped into my mind. "I should have done something for her for Christmas." A wave of guilt joined the sadness. The police car disappeared around the building, heading for the window to pick up the order.

I checked my watch. "Let's wait ten minutes to be sure they're gone," I said to Taz.

"Meow." She curled up on my lap and purred. "I'm glad you're happy to be with me." I couldn't believe how well she had adapted to our crazy situation. I no longer felt guilty about kidnapping her.

Grace pushed back into my thoughts. "Lord, I know I should have done something for her. I guess it will have to wait till I get back. Now please help me figure out what to do next."

I pictured Grace sitting in the carport waving at me. I thought I saw her index finger curl as if beckoning me to come. "I don't remember her doing that," I puzzled.

I felt a strange sensation in my soul. I had felt the same way when God seemed so close, and I felt called into the ministry yesterday. I tried to sit still and listen.

"Do you mean you want me to go to Grace's?" That bony finger curling popped back into my mind. I didn't hear an answer but decided that God was trying to lead me to her.

"But that's back close to the house. I might get caught," I said aloud. An odd certainty came over me. I needed to go to Grace's house.

I tried to picture her house. "Where will I park my Jeep so no one can see it? What if someone spots me on the way in?" Fear and doubt caused my gut to tighten but didn't erase the image of Grace's finger calling me to come to her.

"Trust," was the next thing that showed up in my mind. "Trust?" I said. I felt dense when I realized God was calling me to trust that God would get me there. As I thought about it, there seemed to be enough trees and overgrown bushes that I might be able to park around the back side of Grace's house to be out of sight.

After making the decision to go to Grace's... *well technically God made the decision…* I tried to think through the probable pitfalls. I could see a lot of possibilities: 1. I'd be seen driving into town. 2. I might not be able to get the Jeep sufficiently hidden. 3. Why would Grace let me stay with her for two weeks?

Then a doubt hurt my soul. "What if Grace won't let me in? Taz, I'm not sure this is a good idea. I think we need another plan." She was silent.

"You're not trusting," zinged my heart.

"OK, Lord, if this is your idea then I guess I should just go with it."

I checked my watch: 8:34. It would be close to 9:30 by the time I got to Grace's house. *Maybe it would be better to wait another hour and a half in order to arrive in town at church time.*

"Taz, we have an hour and a half before we head back to Hawksville. What should we do?"

"Meow."

"You're right. I had my coffee treat. It's time for yours." I put six treats on the seat for her and tried to think of something to do for the next hour and a half.

I pulled out my journal to write. It was getting cold, so I wrapped up in the blanket. When I awoke it was 10:23, and Taz was asleep in my lap. I looked around confused, trying to get my bearings. The pieces snapped into place. I knew where I was and where I was going.

"OK, let's go see what Grace thinks about our showing up out of the blue." Taz meowed agreement as I slid her out of my lap then slid into the driver's seat.

I hope I don't scare her. I eased around the side of the house. I probably should have parked in the driveway and asked first, but I didn't want to take the chance of being seen.

When I got to the door, it was already open and Grace was standing there in her hot pink robe, thick white hair flowing over her shoulders. Her deep blue eyes penetrated mine. "Trouble brews, and light does, too," she said, then walked away from the door.

My heart sank as I looked at her back. Then I heard, "And bring the cat."

"Thanks," I said and hurried around to the car. *How did she know about Taz?* I wondered as I scooped her up. "I'll come back for your food and litter," I explained.

I walked in to see Grace setting two bowls on the table. She had already placed two glasses of juice, and I could smell coffee brewing. Before I could tell her I had one more trip, she said, "You don't need it. I have two cats. Show her the laundry room."

I wandered back and showed Taz the fresh litter in the laundry room. *Could she have known we were coming?*

When I set Taz down in the kitchen, she went straight to the food dishes. I noticed there were three.

"You will be hungry," Grace said. "I trust cereal will do."

"That would be wonderful. Thanks!" Grace was already seated, so I joined her.

She closed her eyes, and I could see her lips moving. *She's praying.* I closed my eyes, too. I looked up when I heard her opening the cereal box. Grace guzzled her juice then ate her cereal in silence.

I ate, too, trying to figure out what to say. Two dark gray cats appeared in the kitchen. They seemed to have a sheen on the ends of their fur. I held my breath as they approached Taz.

"Russian Blues," Grace said. "Romeo and Sophie."

"They're beautiful."

"Yes."

I watched as they sniffed Taz. She bristled for a moment then appeared to decide they were OK.

Grace kept eating, and I wondered if she was waiting for me to explain my presence. I glanced at her, and she seemed content. I decided to wait till after breakfast to tell her.

When she took her bowl to the sink, I said, "Grace, I have a lot to…"

"First things first. You'll want a shower." She walked down the hall and returned with a towel and washcloth.

"That would be wonderful."

After the shower and clean clothes, I found Grace sitting in a small study with floor to ceiling bookcases. Books spilled from the cases onto the desk and every other flat surface in the room. She was reading.

"Feel better?" she asked.

"Much."

"You ran away."

"Yes," I answered and began to wonder if she knew everything that had happened since I saw her last. She patted a chair and sat looking at me. *She's ready to hear my story.*

I started at the beginning. "Several weeks ago, I finally realized that I'm…"

"Yes, yes. I know that part. You're homosexual. Why did you run away?"

"My parents want to put me in this place called Sword of Grace so they can make me straight."

"What a terrible name."

She was waiting again. I felt I was beginning to read her a little better. "I drove to Chattanooga and hid out behind a factory. Last night three carloads of guys pulled in, and I ran. They chased me till I pulled into the PetSmart parking lot. Taz and I spent the night at an apartment complex, then a man ran us off this morning. I didn't know what to do, then I felt led to you."

To my surprise, Taz jumped into Grace's lap, and she stroked her back.

"Yes. Darkness. What about the light?"

I was confused. I searched my mind for light then thought, "How could she know?"

"Yesterday afternoon, I felt like God was calling me into the ministry. It seemed so real."

"Maybe it is time. Doors can open."

Chapter 36

Sunday, December 23, 2018

race searched my face with her eyes. "You still have doubts. Will the church accept you? No, it is more primal than that. You wonder if being homosexual is OK with God. Would God have called you to the ministry were it not?"

She seemed to be getting excited. I could hold my question no longer. "How do you know so much about me?"

"I see things. I know things. It makes sense. You are kind. You reached out to me when no one else has. But that wasn't just your doing. God drew you to me for this very purpose. Yes. It is time."

She was out of her chair and running her finger along a shelf of books. I was surprised she moved so quickly. "I haven't looked at these pages in a long time," she said, pulling an old hardcover Bible off the shelf. She pulled a rubber band off it.

When she opened it, I understood the rubber band. Half of the pages were loose and falling out. Sticky notes marked various places.

"Where to start? At the beginning?" She was turning pages carefully to keep from getting them mixed up. She pointed to a highlighted passage. "Read. See things. Know things."

I leaned over so I could see. It was Genesis 19, the story of Sodom. I read through the familiar story.

I looked up when I finished, feeling confused and guilty. *Is Grace trying to show me homosexuality is wrong? That doesn't fit with the reception I've received so far. What does she want me to say?*

She asked, "Does it say homosexuality is wrong?"

"God did punish them."

"Think harder."

I stared back at the passage, thinking about the story. *All the men of the village gathered to abuse the visitors, the angels. In the end, they abused Lot's daughter.*

I thought harder, and a light came on. "These men aren't gay. They left their wives at home and came to abuse the agents of God."

"Good. They just wanted to abuse the ones in their midst who were different. Very good."

My worry receded. She was trying to help me, not change me. Grace turned the pages over to the next marker and pointed.

It was Leviticus 18:22, "You shall not lie with a male as with a woman; it is an abomination." My heart sank. That was very direct. I looked at Grace.

"Read the next verse."

It was about not having sex with animals. I looked up when Grace laughed.

"Can you imagine a woman having sex with a sheep? I don't think the ram would cooperate at all!"

I pictured a woman trying to seduce a ram and ended up laughing, too.

"This passage is from the same section that tells us we can't get a tattoo. That's Leviticus 19:28. Do you think there are any ministers with tattoos?"

I remembered the butterfly tattoo I had seen on the back of Pastor Stevens' shoulder. "I know there are. Our pastor has one."

"What do you think that means?"

"It's OK to have tattoos but not be homosexual?"

"Think deeper. See things. Know things."

I was puzzled. I looked back at the passage and read it again. "Is it saying there are different levels of sin, and we have to rank them that way?"

"You are thinking but not seeing." She seemed to be waiting patiently for another light to come on in my head.

I dug into my mind. "If it's OK to have a tattoo but not be gay, who decided that?" I wondered aloud. "Was it the church leaders?" I stewed until I saw a thread. "We pick and choose what is important to us," I said.

"Light." She was already turning to the next marker.

This was a long passage. "I'll get us more coffee," Grace said. I realized she intended to work at this for a while.

I read through Romans 1:18-32 twice while Grace was gone, wondering what she wanted me to see. It seemed Paul was definitely against homosexuality, but he was also against everything else that the typical human did. But there was that odd phrasing. *What does it mean that they exchanged natural for unnatural intercourse?*

Grace returned with two cups of coffee laden with cream and sugar.

"Umm, that's just how I like it!" I said after my first sip. Grace sipped hers, too. Her bony fingers seemed too frail to be able to hold the cup, but there was nothing frail about her. I was seeing all sorts of life and energy.

"Well?" she asked.

"Back to business. Paul seems to be listing all sorts of sin, here. What struck me as odd was that he said women and men exchanged natural for unnatural sexual relations. It sounds like they were heterosexual and then changed to being homosexual."

"Insightful. Read the next verse."

I assumed the passage stopped at the end of Chapter 1. I continued on to Chapter 2. "Therefore you have no excuse, whoever you are, when you judge others; for in passing judgment on another you condemn yourself, because you, the judge, are doing the very same things."

"That changes the whole passage. Paul was leading up to telling people not to judge others because we are sinners, too," I observed.

"Pick and choose. We pick and choose. Keep reading."

I read on till I came to the part where Paul wrote, "For he will repay according to each one's deeds: to those who by patiently doing good seek for glory and honor and immortality..."

"Paul is saying that God cares about whether or not we do good," I said.

"Like you when you brought me brownies. Good. There is another verse." She flipped to the next marker and pointed.

This one was in I Corinthians. My mind was still dragging through the last passage. *Have I done exactly what Paul said? Have I exchanged being heterosexual for being homosexual?* I noticed Grace was waiting, finger paused over the highlighted passage.

"Questions," she said. I noticed it wasn't a question. I was nervous, but wanted to ask Grace about what I was thinking. *There's no time like the present!*

"I was thinking that it seems like I did exactly what Paul said. I exchanged hetero for homosexuality."

"Did you?"

"It seems like I did."

"Were you?"

"Was I?"

"Heterosexual? Or were you always lesbian and just have discovered that?"

A sense of light poured into my mind. "I think you are right. I had hidden my true self from everyone, including me."

"No exchange. You are now being how you were created to be."

"Yes, that feels right. What's next?" I read through the next passage: I Corinthians 6:9-11.

"That's a nasty-sounding bunch of people. Would Paul see me that way?" I asked.

"Think deeper."

I re-read the passage and puzzled. I thought through the list one by one. "These people are all about self-gratification. They seem to think only of themselves and getting their kicks."

"Truth. The people Paul is describing are not homosexual folks trying to live a faithful life. These are people on a rampage, doing anything and everything to satisfy their desires. We can all do better than that."

I couldn't help myself. It just fell out. I started laughing. Grace leaned back, smiled, and waited. I laughed until tears rolled out. Grace chuckled and waited.

Finally I got out, "I couldn't be a sodomite, anyway." Laughter erupted again. It slowed enough for me to say, "I don't know why I'm laughing so much." A few more chuckles, then I came back under control.

"Laughter is good medicine," she said. "Your heart is catching up to your mind and releasing you from your vexation."

"I don't feel vexed." *I don't think I've ever used that word.*

Grace grinned. "Look at where you are."

I thought again. "I've been the target of attacks at school, my parents threatened to put me in an institution, and I've run away from home."

"Sounds quite vexed to me."

The coffee was long gone, and it was nearly one o'clock. My heart seemed strangely at peace.

Chapter 37

I leaned back in the chair and tried to process all that Grace had shown me. I felt like I had just finished Thanksgiving dinner and needed to be still to digest. Guilt and uncertainty slid out and away.

Grace had gone through the passages that people used to condemn homosexuals and others wrestling with sexual identity issues. She was watching me, sitting patiently with her bony hands folded. Her penetrating blue eyes spoke compassion.

"I now see why God brought you to mind when I had nowhere else to go," I told her.

"The Lord has a way of doing that. I knew you would eventually come to me when I saw you walking to the football game."

"How could you know that?"

"I sensed it."

I wondered about Grace. "Why would she take me in and spend time teaching me? Why did she have all of those passages marked in that worn out Bible?"

That's when it struck me. I didn't dare ask.

"You have more questions." It was a statement.

How can she read my thoughts so clearly? I wondered.

"We need a break," Grace said as she slowly and stiffly got out of her chair, white hair falling forward as she battled gravity to stand up straight.

"Old bones get stiff when they don't move," she said. "You need a rest. I'll show you your bed."

I followed Grace to a guest bedroom, and Taz followed me. Without a word, she closed the door behind me. I suddenly felt exhausted. I hadn't put on my shoes after showering, and there was a throw on the end of the bed. My body felt heavy as I crawled onto the bed and pulled up the throw. I remember feeling drugged just before falling asleep.

A knock on the door dragged me out of a dream. I opened my eyes and wondered where I was. Another knock, and I sat up. The throw brought me back, and I remembered I was at Grace's house. "Come in."

Grace popped into the room. "I trust you had a nice nap."

Looking at my watch, I saw it was two o'clock. A surge of guilt rushed through. "I shouldn't have slept that long."

"You needed it."

Taz rubbed against my leg, and I scooped her up. "Did you have a nice nap, too?" She purred. My stomach stated that it needed some attention.

"I have sandwich fixings out," Grace said.

Taz and I followed her to the kitchen. Taz went to the food bowl, and I sat at the table to create a turkey sandwich. A yummy smelling pot was bubbling on the stove.

"I hope spaghetti is OK for supper," Grace said.

"It smells wonderful."

She came back into the kitchen as I was putting my trash into the can. "Back to the study." It wasn't a question.

We sat where we were earlier, and she asked, "You have seen what the Bible says against homosexuality. What did you think?"

"It mostly referred to..." I was struggling for the word. "Lewd behavior."

"Yes. In biblical times, people saw those with different sexual orientations as evil or perverted. There seemed to be no concept that two homosexual people could care for each other and have a stable, life-long relationship just like heterosexuals. The Bible is obviously against lewd behavior, as you say, but what about those committed relationships that people with varying sexual orientations seek?"

After a few seconds, it dawned on me that wasn't a rhetorical question. "I guess society wouldn't let that happen?"

"Sort of. It happened, but it was kept secret. There are many, many homosexual folks who managed to stay under the radar of the hounds around them. They did what they had to in order to find love and companionship. It was a hard thing to pull off."

Something inside me sensed that Grace didn't seem to just be talking about biblical times. The light came on, and I was certain. *She and Joy weren't roommates. They were lovers.* I no longer needed to ask, but I did ask this, "Is that how you and Joy coped?"

At first I was afraid she would be mad. She smiled, "That's exactly how we coped. People are dense. They never thought beyond the fact that we presented ourselves as roommates. Of course, we had to watch our behavior in public."

"So it really was a sad day when Joy died."

"Yes." That was all she could get out.

We sat in silence. Grace seemed to go to a place far away in her mind. I pictured her and Joy sitting at the kitchen table drinking coffee and laughing. I wondered what Joy looked like. *Will I ever have a relationship like that? It must be hard on Grace living alone and not being able to share her grief. How does she do it?*

I realized I had drifted off in my mind and brought myself back. Grace had tears running down her cheeks. "Are you OK?" I asked.

She didn't respond. I don't think she heard me. I decided to wait for her to come back. The corners of her mouth curved upward in the slightest smile. *Maybe they are tears of joy. She must have really loved deeply to have such powerful memories. I guess that's really what life is about.*

"Pardon an old girl for a walk down memory lane," brought me out of my thoughts. Grace wiped her cheeks. "Now where were we?"

I tried to think back to where Grace had left me. "I think we were talking about Joy."

"We loved each other so much and had a wonderful life together. True to her name, she filled my life with joy. Now my greatest happiness is remembering our time together. But that's not going to help you at all."

"Actually, I think it does. You have shown me what life is really all about. One of my favorite verses is, 'Love one another as I have loved you.' It sounds like that is what you and Joy did."

"Yes, we did. And it made our joy complete. Since you have moved us to Jesus' sayings, what did he have to say about homosexuality?"

"Nothing that I'm aware of."

"Oh, he said plenty, just not directly. As you quoted, he told us to love each other as he loved us. And you know John 3:16."

"For God so loved the world that he gave his only son, so that whoever believes in him should not perish but have everlasting life."

"Whom did Jesus leave out of that statement?"

I had never thought of that. "He said whoever, so that means anyone."

"Absolutely. Jesus loves us all. Do you remember what God said about creation in Genesis?"

"That it was good?"

"Yes. 'God saw everything that he had made, and indeed, it was very good. And there was evening and there was morning, the sixth day.' Did God create you?"

"Yes."

"Then God considers you good! It is human beings who consider us bad, not God. God loves every single created creature on the planet, even the nasty ones. According to anthropologists, homosexuality has been around from the very beginning of human existence."

Grace was on a roll.

"It is not that people of different sexual orientations just up and decide it would be more fun to be that way. It is hardwired into our being, just like heterosexuality is for them. In that case, we have to consider it part of the created order. God made us this way, and we are to live our lives being faithful to Jesus and loving people as he did, just like anyone else."

"You should have been a preacher!" She went pensive for a moment. I had hit a nerve. "What is it Grace? I didn't mean to offend you."

"You didn't. Just another trip down memory lane. I did go to seminary and got my Master of Divinity degree. The church refused to ordain me, though, because I wouldn't denounce my homosexuality or at least keep it in the closet."

"That must have hurt."

"It really did, but I moved on. In a sense, I have been preparing for you my whole life."

Chapter 38

Monday, December 24, 2018

Dim light filtered through the curtains when I bolted upright in the bed. "I don't have a present for Grace, and it's Christmas Eve!" I sat there stewing, trying to figure out what to do. I knew I couldn't risk going shopping.

Maybe she has a box of brownies I could make. I tip-toed to the kitchen and searched the pantry. I was surprised at how well stocked it was. Then I wondered how she gets her groceries. *Does someone bring them to her? Does she have family? Take an Uber?*

It dawned on me how little I knew about her. *I should be afraid to stay here, but somehow I totally trust her.*

I checked the fridge. *Eggs and bacon. I could cook her breakfast.* Checking my watch, I remembered that we ate breakfast around eleven yesterday. *She's not an early bird.* I decided I would shower and dress before cooking since it was 7:40.

Taz rubbed my leg. "You know I wouldn't forget your treats," I told her. I looked over, and two gray hopeful faces were watching. "Yes, you can have some, too."

By the time I showered, dressed, and made my bed, it was 8:30. *Still too early to start breakfast.* I went back to the study to look over the texts Grace had shown me yesterday. Lying on top of the desk and perfectly centered was a letter.

12/23/18
Dear Willow,

I'm not feeling well tonight. At my age, which is 93, one never knows if one will awaken the next morning, so I wanted to share this with you... just in case.

I gripped the paper tightly, and my breathing increased. "Oh, no!"

And just in case, my will is in the top right drawer of the desk. Romeo and Sophie seem to like you. I would be grateful if you would take them and care for them. They are sweet kitties.

First of all, please know that I think you are a very special young lady with great gifts that the church needs.

Secondly, please know that you have chosen a difficult path. The church will not want to accept you until it becomes in line with Jesus' commandment to love each other as he has loved us. As long as it is run by human beings, then human beings will be picking and choosing what they prefer. People will stomp on you as hard as they can. That is not God speaking, but human prejudice.

It was hard to concentrate on the letter. I wanted to run and see if Grace was OK, but I was compelled to continue reading.

Last of all, I lived my life in hiding. It is my one regret. I wish I'd had the resolve to keep fighting and pushing. Joy and I decided we would rather live in peace than be attacked and harassed all the time, so that's what we did. We settled for the water when we were meant for the sky.

As homosexual people living in a world dominated by heterosexuals, most of whom either don't understand or outright despise us, it is always tempting to try to fit in and fly beneath their radar. We try to be feathers in water. I encourage you not to settle for trying to swim when you were meant to fly!

Your Friend in Christ,
Grace

I wiped away the tears and remembered the feather I'd seen floating in the creek. *She couldn't have known about that! No way!*

"I have to check on Grace! She just can't be dead." My mind said, "Go!" but my body seemed glued to the chair. I was afraid of what I would find when I opened her door. It was 8:49 when I finally overcame my inertia and started toward Grace's room.

I opened the door, and she was lying on her back, mouth open. I froze, fear capturing me. Standing and staring, I literally jumped when she snored. Then I couldn't help myself. I ran to the bed, grabbed her in a hug, and said, "Thank God you're alive!"

Several seconds passed before I felt a bony hand pat my back. "Well I guess I am. You found my letter. Sorry if it gave you a fright."

Her voice was raspier than usual. "Are you OK?" I asked,

"I think so. It takes an old woman a while to transition from sleep to awake. It looks like I will be with you another day."

"I'm glad! It's Christmas Eve! Since I don't have a present for you, I'm going to cook bacon and eggs for breakfast. How do you like your eggs?"

"How delightful! I prefer mine sunny side up. And toast. We have to have toast."

"How long till you'll be ready to eat?"

"Give me thirty minutes, please. I'm still not feeling quite right."

"OK, breakfast will be ready in thirty minutes! I left the room feeling relieved. *I don't know what I would have done had I found her dead.* When I came out of my thoughts, I found myself back in front of the desk in the study and sat down to read her letter again.

I focused on the last line. *What would it mean for me to fly? I think I can see myself being a pastor. I don't know about the preaching part, but I've always been told I do well on my presentations.*

A dark cloud came over those happy thoughts when I realized the battles that would have to be fought. *I have a feeling the flack at home and school is just the beginning.*

I looked at my watch and jumped out of the chair. *It's time to cook!*

As the bacon sizzled, I noticed three furry faces lined up. Taz began rubbing my legs and meowing. "So we have some bacon lovers, I see." I added three pieces to the pan for the cats. *It is Christmas Eve!* "Just relax. It will be a minute before it's done," I told the cats.

With the bacon draining on paper towels, I set the table and got out what we would need. *Let's see if Grace is ready for me to cook the eggs.*

I checked the bathroom, but she wasn't there. I knocked on her door. No answer. "Grace?" Nothing. "Grace?" I said louder. I opened the door, and she was still in the bed. I patted her shoulder. "You forgot to get up," I said. No response. "Grace!" I yelled as the reality shook my soul. "Grace! Wake up!" I shook her hard. I checked for a pulse.

Oh, no! What do I do? I tried to remember my CPR class. *Call for help was the first step.* I was grateful there was a phone next to her bed. I dialed 911.

"I think my friend is dead!" I blurted. "I need an ambulance quickly!"

"Can you tell me your address?"

"I don't know the address! I can run look at the mailbox."

"Hold on. This phone is registered to 914 Brandywine Street. Does that sound right?"

"Yes, it is on Brandywine. Should I do CPR?"

"I have an ambulance on the way. If you know CPR, begin now. If not, I will talk you through it. First your friend needs to be on a solid surface."

My mind was racing so fast and time seemed to stand still. Overcoming the fear, I slid Grace's limp body to the floor. She was lighter than I expected. "Come on, Grace! Come back to me!"

I could hear the voice coming from the phone but couldn't understand. I punched the speakerphone button like lightning, then rechecked Grace's pulse. Nothing.

"I have no pulse," I shouted. The adrenaline was at full steam.

"You need to position the person on her back and do thirty chest compressions followed by two rescue breaths. Try to compress the sternum about two to two and a half inches. If you hear a rib crack, keep going."

It was coming back as I was counting compressions. "Twenty-eight, twenty-nine, thirty." I positioned her head and lifted the jaw like the lady was saying on the phone. I remembered to watch for the chest to rise and was grateful when it did.

Back to compressions. "Twenty-eight, twenty-nine, thirty." Back to breathing. Back to compressions.

"Stop and check for a pulse," came over the phone.

"I still don't feel one."

"Continue CPR."

It seemed an eternity before I heard the siren. My arms were so tired. I'm not sure when the tears had started falling on Grace. "I hear the ambulance. Should I go let them in?"

"Yes, make sure the door is unlocked."

I opened the door to see a police car pulling into the driveway with the ambulance right behind it. *Should I run?* The need to take care of Grace quickly erased the fear, and I ran back to her after I knew the officer had seen the open door. *What will they do to me?*

Chapter 39

Everything happened so quickly. I was in a fog. I think it was a paramedic who shooed me away. I remember seeing her hovering over Grace. Then there was a machine, paddles on her chest, and someone yelled, "Clear." I think that happened three times.

The police officer touched my shoulder. "Can I ask you some questions?"

I nodded my head and stood from where I was sitting next to the nightstand.

"Are you a relative?"

"No, just a friend." I hesitated, trying to decide what to say. "I was here visiting."

"What is your name?"

I cringed. *Do I lie or tell the truth. If I tell the truth, they will take me back. If I lie, who knows what will happen.*

Apparently I was staring at Grace while I was thinking, and the officer noticed.

"I know this is hard, but we do need some information to process this case."

Case? What does he mean by case?

"Ma'am, could I have your name?"

He was standing with pen poised over a pad. I told him the truth.

"And can you give me the name of the victim?"

Victim? Does he think I murdered her? Then it felt like a lightning bolt hit me. All I know is Grace.

"I only know her first name is Grace." *That sounds suspicious. Why would I be staying with her if I didn't know her full name?* "I've..." *I remembered her will.* Just a second. I think I know where we can find it."

I hustled to the desk and located her will. "I, Grace Elizabeth Thompson,..."

"It's Grace Elizabeth Thompson," I said, walking back in with the will in my hand. The officer seemed to be eyeing me suspiciously.

"What do you have there?" he asked.

"It's Grace's will."

"I'm sorry, but we haven't been able to resuscitate her," the paramedic said. "I'm afraid she is gone. We will have to transport her to the hospital to be pronounced dead."

She said it with compassion, but the words still hammered me. *How could she be dead? I was making breakfast for her. She seemed OK when I woke her up.* The tears were flowing again.

The officer waited patiently. He was tall and fit and had kind eyes. He handed me a tissue from the box on Grace's nightstand.

"Now can you tell me what happened? How you found her?"

I worked the words out between my tears and told him how the morning went, including finding the letter and making breakfast.

"So you don't live here?" he asked.

"No, I was just visiting."

"How do you know the deceased?"

The deceased? She has a name! "I started visiting Grace after she waved to me while we were walking to a football game one night. She was all alone, so I brought her treats from time to time." I was talking but did not feel like I was in my body.

Everything seemed so disconnected. I realized the officer was talking.

"I'm sorry. What did you say?"

"Do you know if the deceased had family?"

"She never mentioned any, but I don't really know."

"Is there anything else you can tell me?"

"Wait. There is one more thing." I went to the desk and brought the letter she had left me. "She asked if I would take care of her cats."

The paramedics were loading Grace onto a gurney. Her lifeless body just seemed to flop when they laid her down. My heart broke again as they rolled her out. *I can't believe she is gone. I need her!*

"I think we're going to need an autopsy," the officer called to the paramedics as they bumped Grace out the door. I read his name tag: Officer O'Reilly.

Now what am I going to do? I don't think I can bear to stay here without Grace. I need another place to hide. His voice dragged me back out of my thoughts.

"Willow, is there anything else you can think of that might be important to this case?"

There was that word again: case. "No. Like I told you, I woke her up for breakfast, and she told me she was fine. I came in and cooked the bacon and got everything ready except the eggs. When I went back to see if she was ready, she... she was gone." I grabbed another tissue.

"For her to die that quickly, I'm guessing it was a heart attack. Please don't think that we suspect you of murder."

Murder? How could anyone suspect me of murdering Grace?

"I need you to gather your things and come with me," Officer O'Reilly said.

My mind went dark. I couldn't process what he had said. I'm not sure why, but I asked, "Are you arresting me?"

"No. I'm taking you back to some very worried parents. They will be happy to see you."

"No. I can't go back." My voice was nearly a whisper. "They're going to put me in an institution. You have to understand."

"You have to understand. I have to obey the law. I'm required to return you to your parents."

I could run, but he looks like he could outrun me. If I could get to my car... No, he could easily follow me. There is nothing I can do. My heart felt like a stone. *I've lost Grace. Now I'm being dragged back home.*

"Fine!" I stomped to the bedroom and packed my bag. I went through the study looking for Taz. I saw the Bible we had studied from. *I know this is wrong, but I want that Bible.* I grabbed it and put it into my bag. I noticed Officer O'Reilly was positioned by the door. *He knows I thought about running.*

"I'll put this in my car and come back for the cats."

"I'm sorry, but you will be riding with me. I'll take the bag."

I guess I should have realized he wouldn't let me drive my car. "See if you can find cat carriers," I said as I started hunting cats. I remembered the bacon.

Rattling the plates I called, "Here kitty, kitty, kitty. Bacon's ready." All three showed up on cue. I put the goodies down and shut the kitchen door. Officer O'Reilly showed up with two cat carriers.

"I found two." I noticed his confused look. I assumed it was because there were three cats.

Romeo was the first to finish, so I corralled him and backed him into the carrier. He wasn't happy and started caterwauling. Sophie was harder to catch. *You know what's coming, don't you?*

"Don't go anywhere," Officer O'Reilly said and walked out the door with my bag and Romeo. He was back quickly. I had scooped Taz into my arms.

"Anything else?"

"No," I answered gloomily.

He set Sophie in the front seat and ushered Taz and me into the back.

Hope slid away as he backed out of the driveway.

Chapter 40

Monday, December 24, 2018

Slouching in the back of the patrol car, I held Taz close. The sadness and shock of losing Grace mingled with the fear of going home. I began to feel nauseated.

Could I tell Officer O'Reilly I need to throw up, get out, and run? I think I could actually vomit and then run. He would probably keep his distance till I was through. The thought worked its way through my brain until it hit the memory of how fit Officer O'Reilly looked. *He could catch me in ten steps.*

I further deflated and still felt sick. *I learned so much from Grace. I need her to keep teaching me. There is no way I'm going to Sword of Grace. At least I'll be home for Christmas.*

Random thoughts swirled through my mind till we pulled into our driveway. Mom, Dad, and Will came flying out the door. "I guess you told them we were coming." That's when it dawned on me I hadn't said a word the whole trip. *I hope I didn't seem rude.*

I held Taz tightly as I got out and was engulfed in hugs.

"I'm so glad you're home," Mom said. She was actually crying. Dad and Will echoed her sentiment. Taz grumbled at all the closeness.

"Thank you so much for bringing our daughter back," Dad said, shaking Officer O'Reilly's hand. "We've been worried out of our heads."

Will scratched Taz on the head. "We've missed you, too."

Officer O'Reilly was pulling things out of the car. "Here are her bags and one cat. The other one is in the front."

"The other what?" Will asked, taking the first cat carrier.

"The other cat."

Mom took the bag. Dad received the cat carrier, holding it at a distance as if the cat had rabies. I wished I had a picture of his face.

"I have some paperwork to fill out and then I'll need a signature," Officer O'Reilly said. "I'll knock when I'm done." I felt like a Fed Ex package.

I set Taz down on the kitchen floor. She eyed the two cat carriers and went to check on her food dish. Seeing it still full, she headed to my room.

It feels good to be home. I started fielding the questions flying around the room. "Where have you been? Why did you run away? What were you thinking?"

The questions were coming so fast, I finally told everyone to sit down at the table. Then I told the story from beginning to end. When I got to Grace, tears began to flow. I ended with, "We need to let Romeo and Sophie out and show them the litter."

"This is Sophie," I said as I opened her carrier. She darted to the den and behind the couch. "And this is Romeo." He came out and rubbed against my leg. After some petting, he looked around and found the food dish.

"What's with the cats?" Will asked.

"They were Grace's. She left a letter asking me to take care of them, so I am."

"I don't think we need two more cats," Dad said. The daggers I shot from my eyes must have hit home. He didn't say anything else about the cats.

"How did you keep from freezing to death sleeping in your car?" Will asked.

"My car! We have to go get it." *I had totally forgotten about it.* "I had my sleeping bag and a blanket. I stuffed Taz in the bag with me, too. It was actually quite comfy. Will you take me to pick it up?" I asked Will.

"Not so fast," Dad said. "Will and I will get the car. I believe your driving privileges will be suspended for a while. I can't believe you ran off like that."

"I wouldn't have run away if you hadn't threatened to put me in that horrible place!" *Back to reality.* "Have you read what they do to people there? They basically torture and brainwash you!"

"Now, I'm sure it's not like that," Mom said.

"Obviously you didn't read about the program. You were just grasping at straws to try to make me into what you want me to be." I plopped my keys on the table and stomped to my room. *So much for feeling good to be back home!*

Taz was curled on the bed looking happy. Romeo wandered into my room and sniffed around. Duty called, so I picked him up and deposited him into the litter box. He hopped out with a disapproving look.

I got some treats and tried wooing Sophie out from under the couch. I had to toss a couple across the room to keep Romeo away.

"Come on, Will. Let's go get the Jeep," I heard Dad say from the kitchen. It was quiet in the house after they left. I was surprised when Mom set a small bowl of milk down and gave Sophie a call. She came right out.

"You didn't know that I'm a cat whisperer, did you?" Mom said.

"No, I didn't know you had that talent." *What has gotten into her? She is being nice, like she used to be.* I held Romeo back so Sophie could enjoy her treat.

Mom sat down next to me. "I'm glad you're back, and I'm sorry you lost your friend."

"Thanks. She was so kind. She taught me a lot while I was there. I'm going to miss her."

"What do you mean she taught you a lot?"

Oh no! I said too much. Maybe my best option is to just be honest. I took the chance. "She showed me what the Bible had to say about homosexuality and how it is mostly related to lewd, reckless behavior, people getting their kicks however they can. It doesn't really say anything about gay people trying to live faithful lives or in committed relationships."

"I see."

I sensed a door opening. *Maybe she will come around.* "I can show you the verses she showed me, if you like." I held my breath and was afraid to look at her.

I was surprised when her arm wrapped around my shoulder and pulled me closer. Tears were streaming down her cheeks. I hugged her tightly.

"It may take a while, but we can work through this together. I love you and don't want to lose you," Mom said through her tears.

"I love you, too."

Sophie looked up with an expression that said, "Do you mind?" Mom and I burst out laughing.

I knew I might spoil the moment, but I couldn't help myself. "What about Sword of Grace?"

"I think I can talk your father out of that."

It really is good to be back home.

Dad and Will pulled up, and I hurried out to unload my car.

"Wow! That car stinks! Why don't you smell that bad?" Will asked.

"Grace has… had a shower."

The stinky litter went straight to the trash. So did the box. I still had some presents to wrap, so I busied myself with that.

At 5:30, we loaded up to go to the candlelight Communion service.

"I'm glad we are doing this as a whole family," Mom said as we pulled into the church parking lot.

"I am, too," I said, relieved to be with my family on Christmas Eve. "I love Christmas Eve Communion. Everyone standing there holding a candle in honor of the Light of the World is so powerful." Then the thought struck me, *I wonder if they will serve me Communion.*

I didn't think Myra would ever let go of her hug. "You had me so worried! If you ever do anything like that again, I'm going to hunt you down and do you in myself!"

"It's good to see you, too. I'll try not to worry you anymore."

Myra's parents greeted me with hugs, too. *I guess I had a lot of people worried.* A pang of guilt wormed through. We all sat together as a family.

When it came time for Communion, John's family was helping to serve. He pulled the bread dish away from me and went to Will. Will grabbed two pieces, handed me one, and mouthed, "I'll deal with you later," to John.

Kneeling at the altar, I had a strange feeling. I should have been mad, but I felt peace. I even felt sorry for John. *He has some growing to do.*

Chapter 41

Christmas Day had been extra special. Dad had relented on sending me to Sword of Grace – I owed my mother big time – and I had cherished the time with my family. Now we were at Myra's for New Year's Eve. Will had driven me because I was still restricted, partly as punishment and partly because my parents feared I would run away again.

Myra had invited Jaynie, but she politely declined when she learned I would be there. When I found out, it hurt. The pain lifted when Liia walked in. I was so excited to see her. "I missed you!" I said as we hugged.

Liia pulled back and scrutinized my face. "You look OK. I can't believe you ran away. You had me terrified, and there was nothing I could do about it from Upsala."

"I'm sorry I worried you. I just couldn't bear going to Sword of Grace, so I ran away."

"I'm glad you escaped that ordeal."

"How was it being back in Upsala?"

"It was cold and snowy, beautiful! It was fun seeing my grandparents and some friends."

"You're back!" Myra said, rushing up and joining the hug. I blushed when I realized I still had my arms around Liia.

"Hey, Myra! It's great to see you!"

Kyle, Myra's boyfriend, and a couple of others walked in. It was going to be a fun night!

We played Mexican Train, Sequence, and even broke out Twister. At midnight, Myra's parents joined us as we whooped and hollered, "Happy New Year!"

It was during Twister that it finally dawned on me that I was attracted to Liia. Touching her as we twisted around the board was delicious. It was also frightening. *What am I going to do? I don't dare tell her. That might ruin our friendship.*

I wrestled with my dilemma, bouncing from joy to fear through the night. At midnight, we were all running around high fiving, hugging, and ringing in the new year. When I got to Liia, she looked serious. I was worried. *Should I tell her how I feel?*

We hugged, and she whispered in my ear, "I haven't had to courage to tell anyone yet, but I'm lesbian, too."

I think I smiled bigger than I ever have in my life. "I'm so happy to hear that!" My heart overrode my brain, and I said, "I like you… more than as a friend."

"I was hoping that was the case!"

Thursday, January 3, 2019

I'm going on a date! And I actually want to go! I could tell Mom had reservations when I told her Liia and I were going to see Black Panther. I didn't tell her it was a date. I wasn't sure she was ready for that.

Finally off driving restriction, I picked up Liia, and we went to Chick-Fil-A for supper.

"This feels a bit odd," I confided after swallowing a bite of waffle fries.

"How so?"

"I'm on a date that I actually want to be on, for one. And we were friends, now we're dating!"

"I see what you mean. It feels like a relief to me. To tell you the truth, I liked you the moment I met you. I was just afraid to tell you." She took a sip of her soda.

"Maybe that's what it is! A relief! I was a little slower to understand my feelings for you, I guess."

"I'm glad you figured it out."

"Me, too. Why haven't you told anyone you're gay?"

"Are you kidding? I see what is happening to you at school. I'd just as soon avoid that."

"You mean the nasty little messages being left for me?"

"Yeah."

"That is irritating. I wonder if they will start up again when we go back to school?"

"I hope not," she said and placed her hand on mine. I held on and ate with my other hand for a bit. I was happier than I ever remember being.

The movie was quite good. It got even better when Liia reached over and took my hand. We talked and giggled a few times during the movie till someone behind us said, "Shhhh!"

"I guess I should walk you to the door," I said, unsure how to end the date.

"I guess you should," Liia said with a grin.

"I had fun tonight. More fun than I have ever had on a date with a guy," I said as we stopped at her door. She looped her hands around my neck and looked deeply into my eyes. I reached under her arms and pulled her in for a kiss.

My eyes were closed, but there seemed to be light everywhere, like stars dancing in my heart. I felt dizzy when she pulled back and looked at me with a sweet smile.

"Wow!" I said. "I didn't know a person could feel that much at one time!"

"I think you like me," Liia grinned.

"I believe you are right." I said, "Good night," and kissed her again. And again.

"OK, I'm really leaving this time. I'll see you soon."

"Good night," she said.

Driving home, I felt like a new person. "Who is this girl? I don't know, but I'm glad I found you!" I said to myself. By the time I got to the house my smiling muscles were tired from working so hard.

I bounced into the house and found my parents in the den. "We had a great time! You really should see Black Panther. It was fantastic."

They were deep into a movie, so all I got was, "I'm glad you had fun." Romeo was in Dad's lap, and Sophie was in Mom's, both comfortably asleep.

I went on to my room and pulled out my diary, which had been neglected since I got run off from the back of the factory. I grabbed Taz and hugged her before lying on the bed to write.

1/3/19

Lord, you do work in mysterious ways. Eleven days ago I was at my lowest point ever. I had run away and was being chased by a gang of thugs, then run out of the apartment complex where I spent the night. Today I'm on top of the world!

I officially have a... what do I call Liia? Girlfriend? Yes, girlfriend. I had my first real kiss tonight, and it was wonderful! Thank you so much for bringing us together! I can't wait to see her again! Should I call her tonight?

The only dark spot in my life right now is that I miss Grace. Why did you have to take her just as I was getting to know her? She helped me so much. At least her cats seem to be settling in and have won over my parents. I wish I could win them over that easily! I'll have to take letting them know about Liia slowly and carefully!

Then there's the other thing: I have to let them know you called me into the ministry. I'm not sure how they'll take it. I haven't told anyone yet. I trust you'll give me the courage I need when the time comes.

I flipped back to the entry I made when I felt God calling me. *I still feel just as certain that's what you want me to do.*

Deep in thought, I jumped when my phone rang. *It's Liia!*

Chapter 42

Sunday, January 6, 2019

Myra shouted, "Oh, my God! You're serious!" People all over the restaurant looked at us. "That's amazing! First you and Liia, and now this!" She lowered her voice.

Myra, Kyle, Liia, and I were sitting in Steak 'n Shake after youth group, one last fling before school starts back. I had just told them about feeling called to the ministry. "It has been an amazing two weeks," I said.

"We really have to convince Roger to let you speak during Youth Sunday. There is no way we can miss this opportunity." Myra said.

"He's not going to change his mind," I grumped.

"I can't wait to see his face when you tell him you're called to the ministry," Liia said.

"I'm not sure I'm going to tell him."

"We have to. That might convince him to let you speak," Myra said. *She's the eternal optimist.*

"I'm not sure the church is ready for me yet."

"They'd better get ready!" Myra said. *She's more excited than I was about this ministry thing.*

"I'm thinking I should talk to Pastor Stevens first and see how she reacts. I don't even know what I would have to do to become a minister."

"Yeah, start with her, and maybe she will insist that you speak," Myra agreed.

"OK. I'll see if I can get an appointment with her next Sunday." A wave of nervousness oozed through my soul.

✑

Monday, January 7, 2019

Liia and I walked toward school. I decided I would give her a ride to and from school. That would give us more time together.

"I don't think we should hold hands or do anything that draws attention to us while we're at school," Liia said. "I'm afraid it will just cause problems."

It hurt my heart when she said that, but my brain instantly knew she was right. "You're right. There's already enough drama surrounding me."

I fully expected to find another nasty note on my locker. Nothing. There was nothing on Mr. Carlisle's door, either. It was odd that he wasn't in the room.

"Hey!" Myra said as we walked in. "It's time to get cracking again. Five months to go and we'll be graduating!"

Myra was her usual perky self.

"Good. You're here," Mr. Carlisle announced from the door. He was looking at me. "I need to have a word with you, Willow." I joined him outside in the hallway.

"I suspected the people who had been placing the notes about you would try something this morning, so I came in early and kept an eye on your locker. They ran, but I was able to snatch the masks off two of them. They had upgraded to Halloween masks."

I was shaking. "Can you tell me who they were?"

"You'll find out when you press charges, so I don't see any harm in telling you. The two I saw were John Jackson and Wyatt Wilson."

"I suspected them but wasn't sure."

"I'm sure the police will convince them to tell who the third guy is. I hope this will be the end of the harassment, at least these blatant attacks."

"It's hard to believe that people who go to my own church would do such a thing."

"Unfortunately, religion can be used to justify a lot of terrible acts. I don't mean religion is bad, just that some people use it in bad ways."

"I see what you mean." The bell rang, and he ushered me into class. My mind was reeling while Mr. Carlisle took roll. I leaned over to Liia and Myra and whispered that he had caught John and Wyatt putting another note on my locker. They looked disgusted.

I kept zoning out during class. *Why would they attack me like that? I guess they thought they were smart enough not to get caught, but still why take the risk? Did they think they were just playing pranks or are they on some kind of crusade against people like me? How can people like them and Myra exist in the same church? Myra says that her take on religion is that Jesus called us to love each other as he loved us and not to judge. She considers it her Christian duty to care for and affirm people, even homosexual folks. John and Wyatt seem to think their Christian duty is to destroy people who are different from them.*

The questions kept rolling in like thunder clouds. I was so deep into my thoughts that I jumped when my name was called over the intercom. *It's time to make the trip to the office again.*

"Come in, Willow," Dr. Taylor invited. Officer Benefield and Detective Godfrey were in the office, too. When I was fully inside, I saw Mom sitting in a chair blocked by the door.

"Shut the door, please," Dr. Taylor said. "Mr. Carlisle may already have told you that we have identified the perpetrators of the attacks against you."

"He did."

"We brought John and Wyatt in, and they told us the third person is Billy Baggett. It looks like your instincts were right," Dr. Taylor added.

"We will require that your parents press charges against them since you are a minor," Detective Godfrey said.

"And they will certainly be punished at school," Dr. Taylor injected.

I was having strange feelings. I had assumed I would be ecstatic that the people attacking me might go to jail. But now I was conflicted. I wasn't sure I wanted to press charges. *Having a criminal record might ruin the three jerks' lives. Didn't Jesus tell us to forgive each other?*

It came out before I had finished processing my feelings. "Do we have to press charges?" I looked at Mom. She opened her mouth but nothing came out. I could tell she was surprised.

I added, "If they are punished at school, maybe that will be enough."

Mom nodded. "If that's what you want, that's what we'll do. I think that is what Jesus would want us to do."

Detective Godfrey looked relieved. "You certainly have the right not to file charges, but if they continue to attack you, it may be the only way to stop them and ensure your safety."

"I have already called in their parents to discuss what they have been doing and to mete out punishment. We can certainly make them mind their p's and q's for the rest of the semester."

"I want to know immediately if they lash out against Willow. If so, I am pressing charges," Mom said.

Her statement enfolded me in a sense of protection. *Mom is on my side!* I sensed we were back to our normal relationship, and I felt warm and loved. When we stood up to leave, I hugged Mom. "Thanks." She hugged me tightly.

I walked back to class all warm and bubbly. I seemed to have won Mom over. The nasty notes should be stopped. I had a calling in life.

Liia smiled at me when I walked into class. *And I have a girlfriend!*

Chapter 43

Sunday, January 13, 2019

Pausing outside Pastor Stevens' office door, I tried to calm my nerves. She had agreed to meet me at 4:30, just before youth group and the adult Bible study that she taught for parents and any others who wanted to attend. *I'm expecting more rejection, but I have to do this.*

When I raised my hand to knock, she opened the door, startling me.

"Hey, Willow! Please go in and have a seat. I'm just going to freshen up my water."

I went in and was captivated by the books. I was scanning the titles when she walked back in.

"You must be a book lover," she said.

"I am," I responded, trying not to sound too nervous.

"I'm afraid I have quite a fondness for the things. I keep running out of places to put them. Have a seat." She took her place behind the old oak desk, its wood warm and inviting. She pulled back her brown hair and focused on me. Her brown eyes seemed kind. "Now, what did you want to talk about."

I had carefully rehearsed what I would say. "Over Christmas break, I had an encounter with God. I feel like God is calling me to go into the ministry, and I wanted to find out what steps I would need to take." *There, I had gotten that out.*

"Did this happen while you were… away from home?"

How did she know about that? Obviously my parents had asked for her prayers. "Yes, and it was so clear."

"God often seems to reach out to us in times of distress. It seems when we are at our most vulnerable, we are also most reachable. First, you should know that our denomination doesn't allow openly homosexual people to be pastors. It's kind of a "Don't ask, don't tell policy. If you can live with that, then you might have a shot."

"I'm aware that is the case," I said, trying not to let the disappointment show. *Of course Roger told her about my homosexuality! Or maybe it was my parents.*

"To become ordained, a person follows a double process. You have to get a bachelor's degree and then graduate from seminary. At the same time you will go before various committees in the local church and denomination for approval and shepherding along the way.

"I will be happy to guide you through the process if that's what you choose to do."

"I really feel that is what God wants me to do. When would I begin the process?"

"Actually, you just began," she said with a smile. "When I came through, the denomination was still struggling with whether or not to let women be pastors. I have lived some of what you will be facing. But I must warn you, there will be a lot of animosity coming at you."

"I've already seen that. Three guys have been putting up nasty notes about me at school. Two of them are actually church members."

"I'm sorry about that. People become so entrenched in what they think is right and wrong that they can't entertain anything different. I have to confess that I have been ambivalent about having people of different sexual orientations in the ministry. Working with you may help me grow."

Is this really happening? I had expected her to try talking me out of going into the ministry. I was smiling big and tried to look more serious. "What would be the next step?"

"What's today?" she said, looking at her calendar. "Why don't we meet again on Sunday, February third, and talk about ministry, how you are feeling, and bringing you before the church committee?

"I know you probably want things to happen in a hurry, but this is a long process. You'll have at least seven years of college and seminary ahead of you. So just relax and focus on your relationship with God and your spirituality."

"Thank you so much, Pastor Stevens. I'll look forward to meeting with you on the third." I left on a cloud. *I can't believe that went so well! I think she supports me. Uh oh! I forgot to tell her not to mention anything to my parents!* I pivoted and went back to tell her.

"I really think you need to share this with them soon," she said. "It's a big step for all of you."

"I'll tell them after youth group tonight," I promised.

I hugged Myra and Liia before we went into the youth room.

"I'm guessing by your grin that you had a good meeting," Myra said.

"Yep! She did say she was ambivalent about people like me being in the ministry but said working with me might help her grow."

"I hope that doesn't mean she is going to try to squash you down the line," Myra said.

"I don't think so. She seemed genuine. She does want me to go ahead and tell my parents, though."

"You haven't told them yet?" Liia asked, surprised.

"No. Your parents support you. Mine have just gotten over trying to stick me in Sword of Grace. I have no idea what they'll think about my being called to the ministry. Mom does seem to be coming around, though."

"I guess you'll find out tonight," Myra added. "In the meantime, we have to tell Roger."

"I don't want to tell him. He'll just be a jerk." *I know Myra's right, though. She's always right. I guess I'm about due a dose of rejection.*

They were both looking at me, waiting. I sensed Liia agreed with Myra. "OK, I'll tell him," I grumped.

"We'll go with you, if you want," Liia offered.

I squeezed her hand. "Thanks! I'll need some support."

I was nervous all through youth group. Afterward, Myra and Liia flanked me as we walked to the front of the room where several of the youth were gathered around Roger.

Myra, in her mother hen fashion, started things off. "We have some big news! Can we talk to you in private for a minute?"

"Sure," Roger said. He ran a hand through his hair. "Could the rest of you excuse us a minute?"

I could see Myra was bursting at the seams. *If I give her a minute, she might tell him for me. But that's not right.* I summoned my gumption and spoke. "I feel like God is calling me into the ministry."

Roger's face tensed, and he was silent.

"In light of this, I really think she needs to speak at Youth Sunday," Myra added.

He was looking out the window. *Did he even hear us?* Finally he said, "That's interesting... I'm not sure God would call you to something you can't do. The church won't let you be a minister. Maybe you need to keep praying about your calling. It may lead you in a different direction."

Just what I expected. Words tried to explode. I held my tongue and walked away before I said something I would regret. Myra and Liia followed.

"I can't believe that guy!" Liia exclaimed when we were far enough away from the room for Roger not to hear.

"I told y'all," I said.

"Well, at least it's done and we know where he stands," Myra said. "I don't think we can count on his letting you speak at Youth Sunday."

"Yeah, I think you're going to have to give that one up," I said.

"I'm not giving up yet," Myra said. *She is one determined soul.*

Back home, I pulled Will into my room. "Pastor Stevens wants me to tell Mom and Dad about being called to the ministry tonight."

"Good! We need a little drama!"

"What? You don't think they will take it well?"

"Probably at least as well as Roger."

"Yeah, that wasn't pretty."

"I'll be your wingman!"

"Thanks. I can always count on you."

My nerves were ramping up as we sat down to our usual Sunday evening dinner of grilled cheese sandwiches and soup. It was a quiet meal, almost as if everyone was waiting for me to say something.

For the third time today, I steeled myself and cast my revelation into the unknown. "Something happened while I was away from home." Mom and Dad looked up with quick worried faces.

"I felt God's presence in a really strong way." *I think building up to it slowly might work better.*

"That's nice. I'm glad he was there with you," Mom said.

Here goes! "I felt God calling me to be a minister." More silence. I had trouble reading their faces.

Finally Mom smiled and said, "That's nice." She looked at Dad.

He seems… excited maybe? "Does that mean you've decided not to be… you know? Because the church won't let you be a minister if you are… that."

He can't even say the word. "Actually, I'm still gay, and God seems to be OK with that. Grace thinks, thought, the church may be about ready to accept change. She thought it was time."

"I don't care what that woman thought, I don't think it's right. The church doesn't think it's right, either. It goes against the Bible." He hadn't raised his voice yet, but it was coming.

How dare he call Grace, "that woman!" A rise in my voice might be coming, too. "Grace showed me a lot of what the Bible says about homosexuality. Most of it is connected with descriptions of all sorts of lewd and reckless behavior. None of it refers to gay folks trying to live faithful, committed lives."

I could see the muscles in his jaw getting tighter and tighter as I spoke. *Here it comes! You can do that wingman thing anytime, Will!*

"I can't believe my ears! You're trying to interpret the Bible to me? How dare you!" He sputtered over the next words, then got them out. "You're out of your mind if you think I'm going to pay for you to go to seminary on some wild goose chase when I know it will end in nothing!"

"Fine!" I shouted back. "I'll find a way to pay for it myself!" The silence was thick. Will's spoon clinked as he took another bite. *How can you keep eating with all this going on?*

Finishing that bite, Will said, "I, for one, think it's wonderful that Willow has been called into the ministry. I think she'll be great. She's kind and compassionate and will be a great servant. The fact that she is gay shouldn't matter at all."

"I agree that Willow would make a great minister," Mom said. "But I don't believe the church will let that happen. There may be some denominations that would, but ours won't."

What happened next had never happened before. I couldn't believe it. Dad slammed his fist on the table, got up, and went to the bedroom without a word.

"We'll just have to help our denomination see the light," Will said after Dad had lightly slammed the door.

"I wish it were that easy," Mom said. "People just aren't comfortable with this homosexual thing. I'm not comfortable with it, but I'm trying."

"Thanks, Mom. I'm grateful for you."

"Either way, you will have to get your bachelor's degree first, so you will have time to figure out your direction," She said.

"That's what Pastor Stevens said."

"You told her before you told us?" Mom sounded hurt.

"I needed more time to process. Besides, I was afraid what happened tonight would happen."

"Your Dad will come around. He just needs time… I hope."

"I hope so, too."

My phoned pinged. It was a text from Myra. "I have a plan. Get your message ready and sit near the front next Sunday." It was followed by a smiley emoji.

Chapter 44

I hadn't expected to be this nervous. Will popped his head in. "Break a leg! I'm off to pick up Sandra."

"Wait, Will! My hands are so shaky I can't get my necklace hooked." I handed him the little necklace with five pearls. It took him three tries to get it clasped.

"Thanks!"

"Anything for my favorite sister!"

"I'm your only sister."

"That's true, too." He hugged me before rushing out the door.

I know what I'm going to say, so I don't have to be nervous… Yes, I do! I'm petrified! I've never done this before! Breathe. I need to breathe. I took five slow deep breaths and tried to picture a tree with leaves calmly moving in the breeze. The panic calmed.

"Dear Lord, I need your help today. I hope we are doing the right thing." I felt even calmer after that little prayer. *I'll take that as a sign that we are doing the right thing.*

Will, of course, knew, but I hadn't told my parents. I took a seat in the front with Liia and the other youth who weren't in the service, making sure I had the aisle seat. I checked my phone one more time to make sure it was on silent and opened to my notes. It was. Liia squeezed my hand, and my nerves calmed a bit. "Thanks," I whispered.

We moved through the songs, prayer, and offering. Jill and Misty played their guitars and sang the anthem. Their song was inspiring. Roger introduced Myra, who was sitting in the chancel area with the others who had parts in the service.

The nervousness over my message shifted to Myra. *Of course she will do a great job.*

Myra walked to the lectern, positioned her Bible and notes, and looked out at the congregation with a warm smile. *She is always so poised.*

"Good morning! Let me add my welcome to Youth Sunday. We are certainly glad you are here today as we share our faith and ourselves with you.

"It is my honor to be able to speak with you and offer a message that I trust will be meaningful to all of us. Let me begin by reading Luke 6:37-38.

"'Do not judge, and you will not be judged; do not condemn, and you will not be condemned. Forgive, and you will be forgiven; give, and it will be given to you. A good measure, pressed down, shaken together, running over, will be put into your lap; for the measure you give will be the measure you get back.'

"Christianity is an odd religion. Jesus' teachings often are the exact opposite of what our culture assumes is the way things should be. The passage I just read comes from a chapter in Luke that is filled with these types of teachings, teachings that turn reality upside down for us.

" For example, Jesus said, 'Blessed are you who are poor,' and 'Woe to you who are rich.' Again, 'Love your enemies, do good to those who hate you.' Then there is the famous 'Turn the other cheek.'

"He gets totally carried away when he tells us if someone steals our coat we should give them our shirt also. These are not natural things for us. They are the reverse of how it seems life should be.

"That brings us to today's verses. Jesus tells us not to judge or condemn. How hard is that? When we run into someone who is doing something we consider wrong, we want them punished, condemned, judged. When we run into someone who is different, we want to put them in their place, the place we've determined they should be.

"When someone is living in a way that is outside the norms for our society, rather than trying to get to know them and understand them, rather than trying to love them and give to them as Jesus said, it is much easier to judge and condemn.

"I think judgement and condemnation do two important things for us. One, it affirms that I am right, and I'm a good person. Secondly, it gives me a sense of belonging. When I condemn the different, I fit in with the larger group, with people who are doing the same thing.

"What would Jesus say about that? I think he would challenge our attitudes and call us to be his church, a church that gives love, affirmation, and inclusion. That is the hard challenge. It is much easier to judge and condemn than to reach out in love and embrace. But Jesus calls us to take a chance on love, to 'love our neighbors as he has loved us,' to be a people who give rather than judge.

"Will you take up the challenge?

"My best friend has been called into the ministry. She is the most wonderful person I know and has amazing gifts that the church desperately needs. She lives out the passage I read to you this morning. In fact she recently befriended an old, lonely lady whom people at our high school have made fun of for years.

"I think it is only fitting that she come and share some thoughts with us, so I'm going to ask Willow to come up and finish off this morning's message."

I was so nervous my feet felt numb. Liia patted my arm as I willed my body to stand. *I hope I don't trip walking up there!*

The silence made walking even harder. I didn't dare look at Roger's face. *At least he hasn't rushed to the microphone to tell me not to come up!"*

As I stepped into the chancel area, a few people started to clap. Then a few more. By the time I got to the lectern, most of the congregation was clapping. A few more joined in. *Maybe it's peer pressure. I bet Will started it. Or maybe Liia.*

It wasn't a roaring ovation, but I felt supported. I glanced at Roger, and he had a forced smile, clapping weakly.

"Thank you so much. I echo Myra in saying that it is an honor to be here today. I promise we didn't plan this, but my message is based on one of the scriptures Myra referenced in her message. Please hear this reading from John 13:34-35.

"'I give you a new commandment, that you love one another. Just as I have loved you, you also should love one another. By this everyone will know that you are my disciples, if you have love for one another.'

"Let's start at the beginning of that new commandment and ask ourselves, 'How has Jesus loved us?' That's where it begins. We need to understand how Jesus has loved us before we can understand the rest.

"Does Jesus love us only when we are at our best? Does Jesus love us when we are at our lowest? Maybe he loves us in both spots and everywhere in between.

"We live in a small town, so I'm sure most of you know that I recently ran away from home. Taz, our cat, and I were living out of my Jeep behind a deserted factory in Chattanooga. At night, it was very cold. I was using the woods for a toilet. I was alone, down, depressed, and felt totally judged. It was at that lowest moment in my life that God came to me and said, 'I love you and want you to be a minister for me.'

"I felt God's presence in such a real way that I didn't want it to end. When it did, I wrote it all down in my diary.

"I just thought I was at my lowest point then. Later that day a gang of hoodlums pulled behind the factory in their pickup trucks. I was terrified. I cranked the Jeep and took off as fast as I could. They chased me.

"I finally got away from them by parking in a shopping center where there were other people around. After a while they gave up and left. I knew I couldn't stay there overnight, so I found an apartment complex and stayed in the parking lot.

"The next morning I was run off by a resident threatening to call the police. I had no idea what to do. I was parked at the Burger King drinking coffee when God brought Grace to mind. She's the lady Myra told you I had befriended.

"I had taken Grace some brownies and a plate of food. I really barely knew her, but for some reason, God seemed to be leading me to go to her house. So I did.

"I knocked on her door. She looked at me and said, 'Trouble brews, and light does, too.' Then she took me in. Somehow, I knew she would, but still was amazed. Over the next couple of days I discovered she was living out Jesus' new commandment. Myra said I befriended her, which is true. But she loved me just as Jesus loves her."

I got goose bumps when I noticed how tuned in the congregation was. They seemed to be really listening.

"Grace taught me about a lot of passages in the Bible the next day. She helped affirm who I am and the call I had received. She was an amazing lady. The next morning she passed away, and I was devastated. But I cherish having experienced that wonderful example of Jesus' new commandment. My new goal in life is to try to live out loving my neighbors as well as Grace did.

"I haven't been able to flesh out everything about what it means to be called into the ministry. But I do believe that what Jesus wants me to do is simply love the way he has loved me. Don't judge, don't condemn, just love and spread that love to everyone I meet. I think that is what life is really all about. I think that is what following Jesus is really all about.

"I hope you will join me in that journey. Let's all learn to love each other as Jesus has loved us. He said in John fifteen that if we can love each other as he has loved us, our joy will be complete.

"Thank you for letting me share this time with you."

I went back to my seat. The sanctuary was silent. Roger came to the lectern. *I wonder what he will say.*

"As always, our youth did an excellent job today! Let's give them all a big round of applause!" *I wonder if he will just act like this was planned all along.*

"I'm going to ask the youth to line up at the back of the sanctuary just before the benediction so that you can speak to them on the way out. Our closing hymn is number three-forty-seven."

As we got up to walk to the back of the sanctuary, Myra and I were mobbed with hugs from the youth. John and Wyatt steered clear of me. Jaynie came and held out her hand. "I promise to get better. Your and Myra's messages convinced me I have been wrong about this whole thing."

I grabbed her hand and jerked her in for a hug. "I have missed you so much!"

Standing at the back of the sanctuary and shaking people's hands as they left, I realized that Jesus was right. In that moment, my joy was complete.

Books by Shirleen Davies
Historical Western Romance Series

MacLarens of Fire Mountain

Tougher than the Rest, Book One
Faster than the Rest, Book Two
Harder than the Rest, Book Three
Stronger than the Rest, Book Four
Deadlier than the Rest, Book Five
Wilder than the Rest, Book Six

Redemption Mountain

Redemption's Edge, Book One
Wildfire Creek, Book Two
Sunrise Ridge, Book Three
Dixie Moon, Book Four, Releasing late 2015

MacLarens of Boundary Mountain

Colin's Quest, Book One
Releasing 2015

Contemporary Romance Series

MacLarens of Fire Mountain

Second Summer, Book One
Hard Landing, Book Two

One More Day, Book Three
All Your Nights, Book Four
Always Love You, Book Five
Hearts Don't Lie, Book Six, Releasing 2015

Kerrigans of Peregrine Bay

Reclaiming Love, Book One, A Novella
Our Kind of Love, Book Two, Releasing 2015

Sign up to learn about my New Releases:
www.shirleendavies.com/contact-
me.html